You don't need a spaceship or time machine to access my worlds. Neither do you need to find the golden ticket, be the star quarterback or head cheerleader. You just need to grasp the opportunity of adventure and believe in yourself.

Trollrider:
The Last Kriger

'db' Morgan

Megalodon Press

MEGALODON PRESS

Colchester | Essex | UK

www.megalodonpress.com

Megalodon Press: publishing inspirational YA fiction with bite.
Megalodon Press is an independent publishing house based in the
historic town of Colchester, UK.

First published in Great Britain in 2018 by Megalodon Press.

Copyright @ db Morgan 2018

A CIP catalogue record for this book is available from the British
Library.

PAPERBACK ISBN: 978-1-9993491-0-3

EBOOK ISBN: 978-1-9993491-1-0

Megalodon Press is committed to a sustainable future for our business,
our readers and our fragile planet. This book is made from recycled
paper.

Now that you're here, foraging between the covers, inside my world, I'd like to tell you that by buying this book you are supporting a fantastic British charity: The Sick Children's Trust.

The Sick Children's Trust exists to aid the recovery of sick children by supporting the whole family, working towards a future where every family with a seriously ill child in hospital is just minutes from their child's bed during their treatment. Providing free, high-quality, home-from-home accommodation, as well as emotional and practical support for families with sick children in hospitals in the UK, The Sick Children's trust believes that keeping families together significantly improves the recovery of seriously ill children.

The Sick Children's Trust are dedicated to making a real difference to families with sick children. They currently operate ten free-to-stay home-from-home accommodations at major hospitals throughout the UK and are entirely funded by charitable donation.

25% of all 'db' Morgan's personal royalties are dedicated to this fantastic charity. Thank you for helping to support a charity that's extremely close to our hearts. www. sickchildrenstrust.org

This book is dedicated to Jodi.

If I don't tip my hat here to all the people who support my writing ambitions, the Universe won't look too fondly on me. Firstly, and most importantly, my wife, Laura, and immediate family, who trust in my stubborn creativity and stick with me on my journey. You bring me great joy and I hope this book brings you a bit of pride. To my bosses – and patrons – Wesley & Steve at Meatline, who put up with me when I'm supposed to be working, and to my awesome beta-readers and editor. Without your support, guidance and constant motivation Trollrider would never have been born. And for that, I thank you, one and all.

Table of Contents

I am a Kriger. The last one.

My grandfather was a Kriger too. How could a twelve-year-old boy possibly comprehend that kind of responsibility … or the extraordinary danger it attracts? But, if I were to die tomorrow, knowing I, like my grandfather, was fighting for the good of all humanity, I would die with nothing but pride.

My name is Brandon Ballard and I am the trollrider.

Part One

A Boy Impaired

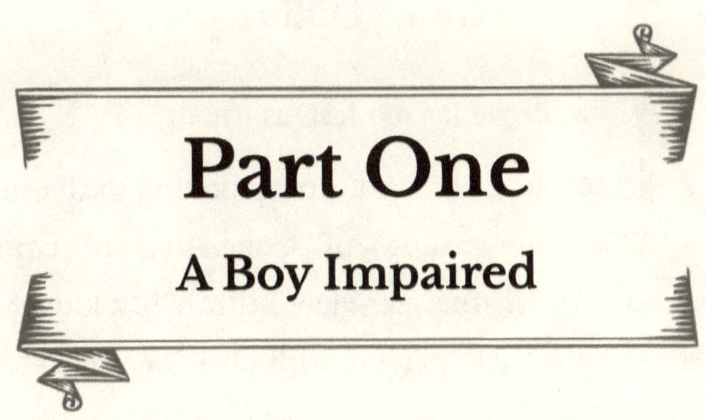

CHAPTER ONE

Going Offline

Mum drove far too fast, as usual.

My anger brewed, slowly boiling to the surface as the shadow of Colchester, of comfort, disappeared through the rear-view mirror. My kid brother sat carefree in the back, playing with his Pokémon cards.

'Are there piggy snorters there, Bub? Oink, oink.'

'Shut up, noob!' I replied, slumping deeper into the passenger seat. I side-glanced Mum, so utterly desperate to get rid of me; to deliver me to the misery and isolation of Pitchbury Farm – the busted-up expanse of mud and broken buildings my grandparents call home. This was the ultimate betrayal!

I checked the speedo: forty-eight in a forty. 'Mum. Please watch the road. Mum, the kerb … The kerb, Mum. MUM!' The speedo crept down to a more respectable forty-three.

'Did you take your meds?' Mum said, then groaned and banged the horn at another vehicle that was clearly doing nothing wrong.

'What do you think?' I replied, contemplating the notion of driving way out of town, to a germ-ridden world with multiple dangers and far too many uncertainties without my medication. 'Shane's mum said I can go to Pontins with them. We can still make it if we turn back,' I begged, pulling out my ace card.

'Grow up, Brandon!' Mum stared at me with the pleading look that stopped working when I was about eight. 'Families help one another. I know it's an alien concept, but let's not make this all about you, eh? Not today.' Mum swerved as the car kissed the kerb. 'You're staying with your grandfather till he's back on his feet. And that's that!'

'And that's my problem because?' My voice pitched up with anger as I touched Mum's wrist, hoping my desperation and anxiety might Jedi-project into her. 'Please, Mum. It's not like any of this is my fault!' In the rear-view mirror, the university towers looming over Castle Park became just a speck in the distance. 'Your dad crashing his Land Rover – not my fault. Breaking his leg and ending up in a wheelchair – not my fault either. And it's certainly not my fault you came up with the stupid idea of me staying there. Instead of you!'

Mum rubbed her temples and shot me a couple of eye daggers.

'It's half term, for God's sake!' I added.

'Don't be such a drama queen.' Mum patted my leg like it was supposed to make it better. 'We'll be there with you for the first week. Besides, you're a strong lad. You'll be loads of help. Sooner there, sooner back, right?'

Mum flashed her fake smile, the one that made my skin crawl. I slumped deeper into my seat, cranked up the car stereo and rested my face on the window – wishing I was someone else.

'Sooner you'll be back more like!' I said under my breath. Mum chose to ignore me. 'You'd rather go to Hemsby with what's-his-face and leave a twelve-year-old to look after your dad. Absolute BS.'

'Well, perhaps you should have thought about that before getting suspended again!' Mum turned down the stereo. 'Am I not allowed to have a life?' Her tone made the hairs on my neck bristle.

'You really don't get it, do you?' Seeing as Mum was salty anyway I saw no reason not to kick back a bit. 'I roll in with a split lip or blood on my shirt and it's all good. Just so long as the little bit of school paper shows over ninety per cent attendance. It's sick, Mum. Would you honestly prefer to see your son get beaten up than lose a couple of stupid bloody attendance points?'

Mum turned away, hit the accelerator just to annoy me, and sighed noisily to emphasise her ridiculous point. It was clear her side of the conversation was over.

I'm not stupid. This was just one of Mum's latest out-of-sight-out-of-mind tactics. One less kid around to chill the feet of her latest grope monkey. And, as per usual, I was the one paying for it. I just wished people would stop treating me like a voiceless little kid. I had my own stuff going on but, apparently, that counted for squat.

Grandpa Dar was a proper old-school tyrant. And a monumental dick. He'd never had a bath, dressed like a homeless and literally hated me.

I took a break from trying to make Mum back down and mentally replayed the time I made Dar try a level on Super Mario World on my old DSi. He'd been digging me out because I couldn't list the names of the birds on the feeder table. I'd laughed at his constant fails till bubbles came out of my nose. But I hadn't laughed when he cupped a fart into my mouth and made me throw up on the new rug. I seriously needed to get Mum to back down.

From the back seat, William snapped me out of my thoughts, stealing my attention by grabbing my ear.

'What's faster of a horse and a tractor?' he shrieked.

I shrugged and turned up the car stereo. Mum turned it down again.

'What's a weasel, Bub?' William's feet began drumming a hideous beat on the back of my chair. I checked the rear-view again. No more proper roads and streetlights. Gone were the familiar supermarkets, skate parks and colourful shop fronts. Just muddy lanes and emptiness.

'Is the farmhouse door strong enough to keep out a angry hippo? Do rats make sense in this world? Do mice eat cats, Bub? Bub … Bub!'

Mum's hand wrestled with mine on the volume knob.

'ARE WE THERE YET?'

I checked to see if my ears were bleeding. They weren't.

William called me Bub and had no volume limiter … just in case you hadn't noticed. It was hideous. And it seriously didn't help when I was at war with Mum and needed to keep my wits about me.

'I want to go home!' I spat the words through gritted teeth.

Mum glared at me with dragon fire in her eyes. 'Change the damn record, will you? Brandon's dragged out of his pit so we all have to suffer! Whoop-de-doo.'

Mum sighed deeply and William copied her. Then he grabbed me from behind. Again.

'I SWEAR, WILLIAM, IF YOU TOUCH MY EAR ONE MORE TIME!' I said, turning to Mum to make sure she'd noticed the hard scowl etched into my face. 'I'm sorry, Mum. I just don't see why I can't—'

'You're twelve years old, Brandon! Twelve. Not eighteen, not twenty-one. Kids don't stay home alone!'

I slammed my back against the seat to shut William down.

'Can you afford twenty-four-seven home nursing till he's back on his feet?' Mum waited for my reply but I chose not to answer. 'Exactly.'

Mum took a deep, stuttered breath.

'I'm not a kid when you want the washing done. Or a free babysitter. Or someone to wait up for you when you stagger in, knock-down drunk.' Mum might have stopped talking but I hadn't. 'You're such a hypocrite! You're leaving me in that crap hole when you know damn well it should be you staying there. Not me, Mum. You!'

I waited for the sting or the backlash.

Mum shrugged. 'Thank you. At least I know I have your support.'

My comment had cut deep – I could tell by the snarky sarcasm and her kicked-puppy eyes. But at that precise moment I truly didn't care.

William started to cry. 'Why doesn't everybody love Dar?'

I looked at Mum. Driving me into the wilderness. In such an epic rush to get her stint of family duty over with so she could escape to Hemsby with her new man. I wondered what it would be like to be taken into consideration. To stand up tall, say no and be listened to. Just for once. William continued kicking the back of my car seat and Mum didn't bat an eyelid.

It must be great being William, I thought.

Looking back, it all seems so strange. This was the beginning of the most incredible adventure of my life, yet at that precise moment I had no inkling of what was to come.

CHAPTER TWO

Forsaken

I remembered the farm being bigger.

Me and Mum had reached something of a standoff by the time we arrived. The silence was uncomfortable, but I was wise enough not to mash her buttons anymore. My anxiety was hovering around five out of ten, and I'd spent the rest of the journey trying to stay grounded. I read number plates and road signs, counted birds, fences, trees; just about anything to keep me from focusing on my inner turmoil.

The forty-minute drive felt like an eternity.

Seeing as we're being open with one another here, I feel the urge to tell you a little about my state of mind at this point. Crippled with worry, in a nutshell. Twenty-four seven. Proper deep-rooted, head-to-toe anxiety! Everyone thinks I'm a wreck. Even my best mates. But I'm not, not really; I just see the world as it is. My eyes are wide open. Though, sometimes, I wish they weren't.

My therapist reckons it came on when my dad left, but I think it's always been there, like a terror worm nestling in my gut, ready to stomp on my confidence every time I take a brave step forward. I try to be positive, I really do, but the world just keeps on crapping on me. I don't particularly like being at home, and school … well … I'm the kid with the invisible target on his back. The one the bullies love the most. The easy mark. And I suppose as long as it's me in the firing line, everyone else is just thankful it's not them. So, as you can probably imagine, it's flippin' great being me.

Mum managed to park the car without hitting anything and William was out before she'd even lifted the handbrake. I'd told her many times to click the child locks on.

'But they're restrictive to a child's development,' she'd say, quoting some specialist or other.

'Tell me that when he's rolling onto the motorway at seventy miles an hour,' I'd reply. That horrific scenario was pretty high on my list of daily worries.

William turbo'd over to Pugwash, the thousand-year-old farm helper who looked like he'd been made out of wet leather. He was directing a couple of men in yellow hard hats as they dragged a huge, splintered telephone pole onto a BT lorry. One lifted William into the cab. Terrible mistake. Before they knew it, he'd locked himself in and was beeping the horn like a madman.

Mum managed to coax him from the truck and we sloshed our way through the mud to the house. I carried my mega-ton suitcase, dragging my feet in angry silence like some kind of slave butler: cold, tired and completely out of ideas as to how to get Mum to give in and save me from a month of hell.

The old wooden front door certainly did look strong enough to keep out the angry hippo William kept going on about, and since there was no way of testing the theory, we agreed with him. Just to shut him up.

Mum grabbed the metal dragon door knocker and banged it hard against the door. The sound rattled through the ancient farmhouse. She knocked again. Then again. Nobody came. So, like the persistent old witch she is, she lifted the letterbox and placed her face against the slit.

'Dad? Hilde?'

No response. I turned back towards the car, immensely relieved that our trip had been a wasted one.

Mum pressed her face up against the filthy window and shouted, 'Hello? Dad?'

I edged nearer the car, my mind drifting off to a fun break at Pontins with Shane and his fam, rather than this punishment – away from safety and comfort, away of my bedroom, my friends, my cat.

The dream was shattered as the letterbox snapped open and the end of a gold club shot out, waggling furiously back and forth just inches from William's head.

'STATE YOUR BUSINESS.' Dar's voice boomed through the letterbox as the metal stick thrashed around wildly.

'Let us in, Dad. It's me, Molly.' Mum dragged William back by the scruff of his hoody. She turned to me, clicked her fingers and pointed at to the door, hissing some kind of mum threat though her teeth. I stomped back to her side, making an obvious show of my frustration.

'DON'T KNOW YOU. DON'T WANT TO KNOW YOU,' shouted Dar, stabbing the weapon through the letterbox. 'Read the bloody sign!'

I looked up and read the notice. No Sales People. The middle word had been scribbled out with red marker pen so it said just No People.

'Dad, it's me, your daughter Molly. And the boys – your grandchildren!'

'Don't believe you. Go away before I set the bloody dogs on you.'

Dar had clearly lost a few more marbles since our last visit.

'Come on, Dad. It's Molly.' Mum leaned against the wall, looking upset. 'Dad, are you okay? Turn your hearing aids up or look through the spyhole or something.'

'Dar, it's me, William. LET US IN … RIGHT NOW!' my brother screeched, fighting Mum's grip on his hoody and clearly amused by the whole situation.

The pole disappeared and I stooped to see my grandfather's crumpled old face on the other side of the door.

'Is that you, my little habbadehoy?' Dar bellowed. 'Show me your eyes.'

William crouched down by the letterbox.

'And the rest of you!'

One by one, we showed our faces through the letterbox.

'Open the door, silly. I need a poo,' William said.

'What's the magic word?' the letterbox replied.

'PIFFLEBUNK!' said William.

We waited.

One lock opened, then another, then another. And then one more. Dar's front door had more locks on it than a bank vault. It took a whole minute before the door swung inwards and then, unfortunately, we were in.

My new kicks were caked with mud and I spent my first ten minutes in the farmhouse on my hands and knees, scrubbing the kitchen floor, Dar looming over me in his wheelchair like a Dalek.

Like he was still in the army.

Like a total dick.

Dar was almost eighty years old but he was still all about authority and correct behaviour. The exact reason why being here was one of my worst nightmares … possibly even worse than having to be around Aiden Hunt, my nemesis. At least at school I could run away and hide in the art cupboard, or take a couple of hits, wash away the blood and wait for the bruises to go. But here I was trapped. Not even a school bell to rescue me at the end of the day.

Trapped in the land of crap and mud. Great! Thanks, Mum.

Our first dinner was a highly memorable event for all the wrong reasons. Nana Biddle, or Old Whippet Legs as I preferred to call her, threw her teeth at Wrigley because he stole a lamb shank off the table. We spend two hours searching the barn for them in the freezing wind.

Wrigley is their big, slobbering, lurcher dog, and Nana Biddle was possibly the craziest person I'd ever met. She'd once been quite a famous opera singer apparently, but now spends most of her time gluing buttons to the trees. Nana Biddle was off the scale. And I'd never known her any other way. Anyway, best explain that right off the bat, because normal people don't throw their false teeth at dogs when things don't go to plan.

Mum would certainly have her work cut out for her over the few days.

-db- Morgan

Good!

It was nine o'clock before I managed to escape to my room, and by that time my anxiety monster had gifted me a hideous headache. I took six big drops of Rescue Remedy. It wasn't enough.

'Where did you pack my sertraline tablets?'

Mum ignored me as she folded my T-shirts and placed them in a scratched-up old wooden chest.

'Mum, I need my tablets. Please!'

She tutted and slammed the drawer shut. 'Ride it out till morning,' she said through clenched teeth.

We'd played this game a thousand times and, like a Wild West gunfight, the first to draw won. I thought I'd worn her down on the journey here, but Mum was clearly sticking to her guns today.

'Please don't bother unpacking my stuff. I can do it myself.'

Mum hmm'd as if to say, *You can but you won't.*

'Shane's Mum said they can pick me up on the way to Pontins. The one with the new water park. The one in the brochure you promised to take us last year ... *and didn't.* Please, Mum!' Yep, I was begging ... but the embarrassment of showing weakness was nothing compared to the alternative.

'ENOUGH!' Mum turned and loomed in front of me, hands on hips. 'Listen to yourself. Me this, I that. In case you hadn't noticed we're all out on a limb here, but you don't hear me complaining, do you?' Mum was fuming. I'd finally hit the monster button and an explosion was close.

'I just want to go home, Mum.'

Mum sat on the bed – a cloud of dust rising around her butt – and patted the hideous, itchy patchwork blanket next to her.

'I know you're struggling to deal with this, Captain, but please, please, I need you to be the man here. Can you do that … for me?' She pulled me close and kissed my forehead.

Okay. Pause. I'm not afraid to admit that I cried a bit. Because I wasn't at all comfortable with new situations, with change, and certainly not with being away from my bedroom, my friends and my cat – essential home comforts – for such an unspecified period … and against my will.

Mum hugged me for the first time since I could remember – for a solid minute, too. And then she left to cook the tea.

I'll miss Lil the most – my fat, useless cat.

And I absolutely am *not* going outside unless the world's on fire.

CHAPTER THREE

I Am NOT Jealous!

Everything's wrong here. The smell, the internet, the food, the people, the way the time passed. Even the ground was wrong. And as for the furniture, well, that not normal either – all fancy curls and twists of wood and pads of material. When you plonked down on them a fart of dust flew everywhere. And the windows were leaded with big grey metal diamonds all over the glass – like prison bars.

I dragged an old chair over to the window and climbed up into the bay. I was greeted by an ocean of dead flies on the sill. A fat, crispy bumblebee lay in the middle, on its back, like an island. I could see right down the yard. Even though there were no streetlamps here the moon did a good enough job of helping out. The horse stables on either side, then the big old barn, and a building that had once been the milking parlour, and then beyond that, the orchards. Mud, more mud and broken wood pretending to be buildings. And I'm the one who got shouted at for letting my trainers bring a bit inside.

There are loads of stars here. Thousands of them. It seemed dumb to me that they only came out in the country when they'd have brightened up the towns no end. (Just my little joke! Tra-la-lah. Astronomy's one of my happy things, and the main reason I was choosing science as an option.) The stars pierced the pitch-dark sky like diamonds. Clean air and no light pollution – a perfect recipe for a starlit sky. So that was one positive. Being away from the smog and grime of the town might give my allergies a rest, though knowing my luck I'd be allergic to mud and chicken crap.

The longer I looked out into the night the better my vision became. Way beyond the orchards, what I'd first thought were dark clouds were actually huge trees. I figured it must be Pitchbury Wood – one of the old forests of England, and supposedly home to Boudicca during her invasion of Colchester, or Camulodunum as it was known in Roman times.

It was huge, it was full of nature and it was boring. I vaguely remembered Dar taking me up there once when I was William's age, to show me how to catch fish with my bare hands, but I don't remember finding the stream; just another lecture.

I stared at the stars for a bit, watched a rat dragging a cob of corn across the yard, and then got scared when I heard a wolf cough in the distance. I gave Crispy Bumblebee my best Harry Kane rocket flick and it exploded spectacularly against the window.

And that, my friend, was the highlight of my day!

Me and William used to be tight.

He'd listen to everything I told him and be quiet when I spoke. That was the cool part because I taught him all the important things, so he'd grow up just like me. I taught him how to burp and whistle and do an ollie on a skateboard. I showed him how to play *Fortnite* and do front flips on the trampoline. And I'd tried to make him strong and fearless and optimistic. Not worried about every little damn thing. Basically the opposite of me. Which makes your head hurt twenty-four seven, trust me!

But he's just turned six and something's changed.

He is absolutely relentless. I was that sure if Mum had bothered getting him tested he'd be diagnosed with something like Asperger's or ADHD. It's not that I don't love him. Maybe it's because I'm older now and have more responsibility – looking after him and doing stuff around the house, while he seems to be able to do whatever he likes.

And I'm the one who gets to live with the consequences. I know this makes me sound like I was an epic hater, but I'm not. Not normally anyway. I was fine when I was safe at home, but at this point that's exactly where I wasn't. And I don't think you'd have been fine either if you'd been in my shoes.

I heard voices from across the hallway. William and Dar. I'd never understood why they got on so well. My little brother had stayed here loads of weekends over the past few years while Mum was away doing God knows what with God knows who, just to avoid being at home. So I suppose they'd built a relationship. And whoopee for that!

I slid out of my room and hunched down by the door. It was open, just enough for me to peek in but remain out of sight. I listened. Not that I was interested in story time, honestly. I'm twelve and three quarters! I just don't like being alone with all the creaks and dark corners. And I certainly didn't want Dar and my lil' bro to know I was tucked away just outside the room.

William poked Dar's face.

'Why have you got brown spots on your face, Dar?'

'Because I'm so very very old.'

William chuckled. 'Like a rotten apple.'

'Hmmm, something like that,' Dar replied.

Dar raised a small children's book. 'The farm mouse scampered up the rope, chased to a hair's breadth by the big fat tomcat.'

William groaned and pushed the book down on Dar's lap. 'This story's for nappy babies. More secrets!'

Dar shushed William and glanced towards the door. In the distance, the old church village clock began its hourly strike.

One, two, three …

'Bedtime stories for babies? Pifflebunk!' Dar sounded irked.

Four, five …

William shrugged.

Six, seven, eight …

William yawned loudly.

Nine, ten.

It was ten o'clock at night and William's engine was still red-lining. At least Dar could now see why I got so irritated.

'Does Mummy not read you stories then?'

William shook his head vigorously.

'Then maybe Mummy's a smelly-nappy baby!' He poked William in the ribs a few times and William curled up like a hedgehog, chuckling. 'Well, it seems I underestimated you, my little habbadehoy. You are almost ten after all!'

'I'm six, silly!' said William, though I could hear the pride in his voice from the compliment.

'Well, okay then. No more smelly-nappy-baby stories. You want a proper grown-up story. Are you ready for the superest, most super-duperest story?'

William jumped up and down on the bed excitedly.

'Then settle down, little bean. You asked how I broke my leg, so I'll tell you. But if, and only if, you can remember the Kriger promise.'

'Erm. I will not speak?'

'No. I will not tell,' Dar said.

'I will not tell. I will not speak, or else I'll lose my tongue or feet,' William said. It was like when they made us say the 'promise' at cub scouts. 'And if I speak or talk or tell, then Dar will throw me down the well.'

'And then we spit and we shake!' Dar completed the weird ritual.

I rose quietly and leant on the doorframe, finding my balance. I was bored and tired, and had to help fix that stupid bloody chicken fence in the morning.

'Okay then. No more smelly-nappy-baby stories. Seeing as you're a grown-up six!'

William sat up and wrapped the blankets tightly around his chest.

'I am a robot!' Dar said in his best automaton voice. 'They chopped me open and fixed me up with robot parts. Like the six-million-dollar farmer. I've got robot legs, robot knees and eight metal rods and plates in both legs. I've even got a robot hip bone. And so, you see, I am now a robot farmer.'

'You're not a robot, silly. You're made of skin and blood.'

'Am too! After the crash they took me to a special, secret hospital in the middle of the city and turned me into a turbo farmer.' Dar leant into William and lowered his voice to a whisper. 'So I can keep the bad men away when they return.'

'Were you scared for real?' William clapped his hands, totally hooked. And I too was paying close attention to the crazy story.

'Terrified. And if it hadn't been for Wrigley – the finest Kriger hound there ever was – sounding the alarm, they'd have won.' Dar leaned into William and whispered, 'And I would have failed in my mission. Oh, it was a frantic battle, my little habbadehoy. They came in great numbers in the dead of night, up on Flossy's Field, and I smashed up their trucks with my Land Rover. Four, five trucks of men, racing across my fields while the moon was high.'

'But you Hulk-smashed the bad men all up. Yay.' William was hyper given the time of night, but it was a great story, and Dar, for all his faults, was an awesome storyteller.

'Nope, they Hulk-smashed me all up. Flipped my Land Rover upside down and smashed me up from all sides. Until Forfaltrot swung in like Tarzan and swatted the bad men away with a telegraph pole. Swish, swoosh, smash. He ripped it right out of the ground with his bare hands and swatted their trucks away … like flies. Like they were nothing. He absolutely saved my skin. And we lived to fight another day.'

'Good old troll!' William leaned closely into Dar, utterly captivated.

'But now I'm a robot. Next time, they won't be so lucky. We'll force them off the farm, before they even get close to the fields. Never to return.' Dar sighed deeply and William yawned.

'Trolls don't really make sense in this world. Not for really real,' William whispered.

'Don't they now? Trolls are beings of nature,' Dar said. 'But they do have natural urges that must be curbed … like you, William, with your urge to screech and colour in the walls. Come!' Dar wheeled himself towards the window using his upstairs wheelchair. William scampered after him, climbed onto his lap, and hoisted himself into the window bay.

'You see that big spike way beyond the orchards?'

William pressed his nose against the glass and nodded.

'Well that's the church spire. Do you remember? I took you there last harvest festival.'

'Huh?'

'And Father Ball gave you the little pink sugar mouse.'

William began bouncing and squeaking. There was nothing like a sugar-loaded treat to help William recall an occasion. Dar held him still, probably worried he might smash his head against the window.

'And inside is the church clock. And right at the top of the spire is a mighty bell.' Dar plucked William from the window bay, rode back to be bed and moved him gently onto the covers.

'WHEEE!'

Dar shushed him and glanced towards the door. I froze, wondering if he'd seen me.

'It is an absolute fact that trolls find the sound of bells obnoxious. So, every night, for the past few centuries, all the church clocks in rural areas ring out the villagers' warning: *Leave our land. Leave our people in peace.*

I admit it – I was utterly transfixed by Dar's story. I hadn't reckoned he'd have a clue about how to talk to a boy of six but he held William's attention all the same. And mine! It was nice. I couldn't remember the last time anyone had taken the time to read to either of us. Maybe this is was what normal looked like.

'Fetch me the atlas.' Dar waggled his finger at a dusty oak bookshelf in the corner of the room, stuffed with old books. 'Left, down. Left. LEFT. Hell's bells … I'll fetch it myself.'

William hopped back into bed, clearly upset.

Dar wheeled back towards the bed with the atlas. 'Look.' He held up his hands, palms facing outwards, fingers vertical and thumbs at ninety degrees. 'It's an L shape. L for left. See?' William nodded. 'Clever boy. See? Just nobody's shown you yet.'

Dar opened the atlas and thumbed through a few pages.

'And I know all the Pokémon! Like Pikachu, Eevee, Snorlax, Dragonite, Pichu, Mew, Jigglypuff, Psyduck.'

'What a lot of colourful names. What's Pokémon?'

'You're funny,' William said.

Dar drew William's attention to the map. 'The Norse settlers in Orkney and Shetland.'

'Marowak, Gastly, Muk, Ditto, Charmander.' William marked out the names on his fingers as Dar gripped my brother's head and turned it back to the pages. I couldn't see over my grandfather's shoulder but I was pretty sure he'd be cringing right now.

'The Norse invaders brought trolls with them … used them as weapons to defeat the armies of England,' Dar continued. 'They chained them, tied 'em up tight so they were powerless, and kept them in the hulls of their mighty *langskips.* That's their ships.'

William snuggled into Dar.

'And Snorlax. I like him because he's fat. Like Bub's cat.'

Dar placed his hand playfully over William's mouth. 'And when the winds lulled, the mighty trolls were wheeled out to bellow the sails.'

William was suddenly wide-eyed and attentive. 'But why would they want to help?'

'They didn't,' Dar said. 'The *Heksejeger* poked them with spears and used the trolls' mighty roars to power the sails … and as *battle cries* … to strike fear into the hearts of the enemy. Do you know the meaning of the word *Heksejeger*? It means witch-hunter.'

'Witches!' William screeched.

'I thought that might catch your attention, my little habbadehoy.' Dar's voice grew softer as he reeled William deeper into the story.

'Can I get taken by a troll, Dar?'

'No, you misunderstand me, little bean. Trolls are goodies. Trolls are the best.' Dar lowered his voice to a whisper. 'That's why we protect them from the bad people. They are misunderstood magical beings from a different time. It's the *Månejegere* and the *under-skjult* we need to be truly afraid of. But that's a whole different story for another day. Tomorrow, I'll show you the secret map. Would you like that?'

William nodded enthusiastically.

'Now, time to sleep.'

I scrambled to attention and sneaked across the hall as Dar flicked off William's light. Then a thousand stars filled the hallway as William turned on his starlight turtle.

I tiptoed into my room.

'Brandon? Is that you?' Dar called from William's room. He sounded shocked.

I clicked the door shut and jumped into my cold, lonely, bed.

Dar's finger rapped lightly on the door. 'Night, Yormagorp.'

'Goodnight, muckheap,' I replied.

Dar opened my door and entered. 'You … er … enjoy story time?'

'Don't know what you mean,' I said politely, pulling the covers over my face to hide the lies.

'Earwigging! That's … your little brother certainly loves a tall tale or two. Did you, er … did you enjoy the story?'

'I wasn't really listening to be honest. I was just charging my tablet at the socket. He's like six. And I'm almost a teenager.' I wasn't a huge fan of lying, but needs must, and I certainly didn't want Dar to know I liked his baby stories.

'Good for the imagination, stories. Tall tales and ripping yarns.' Dar drummed his fingers on the door, clearly uncomfortable. 'Good old stories for nimble minds, my little habbadehoy.'

'I know, Dar.'

'You sleep well, boy,' he said, and closed my door.

'You too, Dar.' I listened as he clambered from his wheelchair and hobbled down the stairs on his crutches. The creak of the wheels from his downstairs wheelchair faded away as I drifted off to sleep.

I dreamt. A heart-thumping dream. The kind of dream heroes have! And instead of a usual night of broken sleep and worry, my mind transported me to a different place.

I was living in the forest, at the base of an old oak tree. My bed was lovely and soft, made from sacks and hay. A burning fire lit my camp. A sentry tower, traps and trip wires would alert me to imminent danger. And I was free. With no stupid, unnecessary rules.

Then came an earthquake, and with it a mighty storm and a horde of evil men. Terrifying men hell-bent on kidnapping me because I'd discovered a deadly secret.

They chased me through the storm, but as much as I shouted at them to leave me alone, my little voice was lost to the howling winds, and they pushed on.

My awesome gun – like the legendary assault rifle, SCAR, from *Fortnite* – was useless. The bullets turned into caterpillars and squished into toxic sludge when I tried to load them into the clip. I screamed and shouted, making myself as big and loud as possible to scare them away.

I was terrified. Powerless.

Then Dad showed up and saved me by leading me into a secret tunnel under the forest floor.

Because that's what dads do.

It was incredible. One of those dreams you could smell, touch and feel. The kind of heart-pumping dream you didn't want to end.

CHAPTER FOUR

Thirty Acres of Mud

'School's not going too well, I hear.' Dar hammered a rusty old nail straight on a concrete slab perched across the arms of his wheelchair. He held up the straightened nail for my approval.

I shrugged. 'Meh.'

'Never waste anything. Knock 'em straight … good as new. Perhaps I should knock you straight.' Dar smiled up at me, possibly expecting formal praise for his wit. 'You've been fighting again. And skipping school.' He raised his eyebrows and cocked his head towards me. Hideously patronising! 'Hardly the most intelligent of choices, Brandon.'

'If you call two idiots holding you by the neck while another smashes your guts to pulp then, yes, Dar, I've been fighting.' I passed him a few more nails. My fingers were frozen purple and I feared they might fall of at any minute.

'You can't solve problems with your fists, boy. You're smarter than that. If you've got problems, speak to your teachers.' Dar straightened out the nails and held out a hand for more.

'Why d'ya think I bunk?' I dumped a huge pile into his lap, desperate for this horrendous chore, and the accompanying lecture, to be over.

'So, either way the bullies win. Surely there's one teacher you can trust. They *will* help you deal with it. It's what they're there for, Brandon. You won't get a second chance at a good education.'

I snorted at his stupidity.

'Like you understand. I'm sure things have changed quite a bit since you were at school.' I dropped a couple of nails into the mud and scuffed the front of my trainer over them. I really did want to tell Dar everything but knew nobody could fix my problems, least of all an eighty-year-old farmer.

'They've got security guards now. With metal detectors so they can do knife checks.' I stared at my grandfather and waited for a reaction that didn't come. 'Kyle Weston, from year nine, was expelled last week for selling cocaine behind the IT block. Cocaine, Dar. Class-A drugs and knives. That's what education is now. Teachers only care about targets. Ticking boxes, hiding from the truth and giving treats to bullies and idiots.'

Dar put the hammer down and looked at me.

'And they certainly don't care about kids like me.' I blew on my hands and hoped he'd see I wasn't exaggerating.

'So you skip school? Get into more trouble? Fall further behind with your studies? Then what?'

I grabbed another pile of nails and handed them to him.

'Like I said, you wouldn't understand,' I said, severely gutted that I'd wasted yet another hundred words or so on such unsympathetic ears.

My section of fence was deep inside the birch hedge and I had to twist bits of wire around every hexagon of ripped metal and then fix it with a nail. It was horrible. And to make things worse, there were millions of spiderwebs. Dar was on the other side, but still close enough to force his lectures on me. The ones that Mum had clearly puppeteered. What it boiled down to was basically this: I'm a problem child on the threshold of being sent away to boarding school. Mad, right? I was the one being terrorised at school. I was the one who saw the world a little more clearly than all the morons on the planet. And I was the one worrying about it far too much. But yet again, I was the one being punished.

As I said, it was flippin' great being me.

God knows how the fence had got so mangled. I even found bits of hair and blood, that Dar told me it came from foxes. They must have been ninja foxes on stilts who'd rolled in rotten eggs because it stunk! But what did I know? I was just a maladjusted town rat. *Apparently.*

What I did know for sure was that it was late autumn, my lips were cracked and the veins in my hands looked like blue cheese.

'Did you know that foxes are distant relatives of wolves?' Dar called across to me.

'No, but I heard one cough the other night,' I said.

'You mean a fox. And foxes bark,' said Dar.

'Nope. It was definitely a wolf. Far too loud to be anything less. Unless it was a troll,' I said, deciding to ride him a bit.

'I'm sure you didn't. There are no wolves in England anymore. You should know that. And there certainly aren't any trolls.' Dar seemed disappointed with me.

'Sure sounded like a troll, Dar. Came from way across the field. Pitchbury Wood maybe. A huge bellowing cough … no, a mighty roar, like a battle cry.'

'You're mistaken.' Dar spat on his hands and rubbed them together. Gross!

I laughed. 'Must have been a troll – a big hungry one! You should have turbo'd over there on your robot legs and taken it for a ride.'

'It wasn't a bloody troll,' Dar snapped. 'They don't exist. And it certainly wasn't a wolf either. So keep your half-witted thoughts to yourself.'

I was a bit shocked that Dar had got all bent out of shape. Part of me wanted to shout back and quote his troll story to William but I was too cold to bother. Rude, cranky old man! I'm not sure what school of motivation he'd attended but I couldn't imagine it would be considered acceptable by today's standards. I wasn't even sure that Dar had gone to school. Had he meant to lecture me? Probably not. Maybe he was just trying to be a father figure after Mum had been all up in his ear like a wasp.

Still, I was learning something – maybe his gruffness was just be for show. Some kind of banter or bluffery to hide the fact he wasn't so cruel after all. I decided that the problem was we had nothing in common so he uses every single opportunity – like today – to teach me about *proper* things like toolsheds and tractors and socket sets and gentlemanly conduct. But what was the use in that? How would any of that country-bumpkin malarkey improve my life? If he truly wanted to help he could come to my school and run *Aiden Hunt* down with his combine harvester, or get Mum to spend less time out clubbing and snogging idiots. Real-world problems!

When we were almost done, I tested my theory by calling him the F-word that begins with W. He proceeded to rub a wet pile of chicken crap in my face.

Maybe he was an idiot after all!

I'll probably never find out the answer to that one, but Dar had certainly got sand in his vag when I'd dared to mention the T-word. His reaction to my mention of trolls had been waaay over the top.

I decided, there and then, to pay more attention to lil bro's bedtime stories.

CHAPTER FIVE

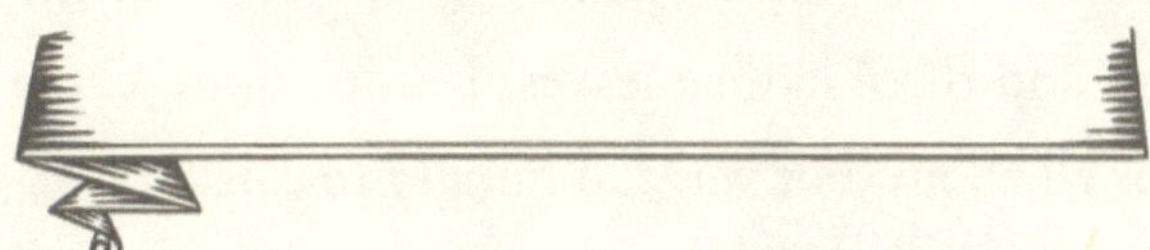

Don't Go into the Toolshed

We'd fixed the chicken-paddock fence and I was not happy – not at all. I was cold and tired. And tomorrow or the next day, Mum would be leaving and taking William with her, acting out happy families with some new moron who'd be playing dad to William for a few days; just to get into Mum's good books … and other less educational places.

I would be alone.

I tried not to let it consume me, but it did anyway. It wasn't right but was happening all the same. I had zero control, and my only shred of comfort was that William would be going back to school and I wouldn't … for the time being. It absolutely wasn't my fault I'd been suspended, but I was being punished all the same.

I was destined for a different kind of schooling, sentenced to be Dar's fart-catcher. Gross, I know. That's what they'd called footmen and butlers back in his army days. I'd definitely have preferred 'trusted helper', 'personal assistant' or 'epic muscle manager', but unfortunately 'fart-catcher' stuck. Yet another thing I had no control over.

Lunch was a boiled egg wrapped in squashed sausage hidden inside dirty breadcrumbs. It was served with some cold fish and three lettuce leaves. I didn't quite know what that was all about, but was too hungry to care.

After we'd eaten, I wheeled Dar to his toolshed: a huge slopey-roofed building glued onto the side of the farmhouse. It would have taken William about twenty seconds to run the length of it, but you can't run in there. Can't touch *anything*. Can't even sneeze.

'This toolshed holds over a hundred years of usefulness!' Dar explained, clearly excited to introduce me to his workshop. 'A thousand shelves and pigeonholes, each with something utterly unique and interesting inside. Any repair, project or emergency … it's all here, my little habbadehoy.'

At home we had one hammer. Here you could spend half a day choosing which one to use. It was weird seeing Dar so animated over something so rubbish. Literally. There was rubbish stuffed into holes and rammed onto shelves. Crap stacked upon crap stacked upon crap. Buckets of rusty nails, broken tools, everything! Dar's toolshed was like the Junk Lady's house from *Labyrinth* – one of my absolute favourite films. I loved movies – the perfect short-term escape from reality. I must have watched that one over a hundred times. (If you haven't seen it, make sure you do. It's totally epic!)

Something else – I'd never seen so many cobwebs in one place in my entire life.

In the middle of the toolshed, next to a massive saw built into an old table, there was a something covered in a sheet. Dar whipped off the wrapping, full of pride.

'Introducing the Galloping Goose!' Dar waited for some kind of reaction.

'It's another wheelchair,' I said politely. This one, however, was utterly ridiculous. Dar pointed excitedly, like he was 'Doc' Emmett Brown from *Back to the Future*. (Another one of my top-ten movies.)

'Fat wheels from an old barrow … the arms from a Parker Knoll armchair. And this … this was my father's, *your great grandfather's*, old shaving mirror. And now it's fixed to the end of a golf club. Everything recycled. Marvellous, isn't it?' Dar swung the mirror around to demonstrate – presumably so he could force an eye-to-eye lecture onto his poor chair-pusher.

I wasn't sure what kind of reaction he'd been expecting. The evidence was there for all to see. It was a bat-crap crazy contraption, literally held together with glue, gaffer tape and cable ties. A tea-cup saucer had even been stuck to one of the arms. It was the creation of a madman.

Then my attention was drawn to one of the tucked-away boxes in a cubbyhole to the side. Something far more interesting poked out from the top.

I looked over to Dar as he squirted oil onto the wheels of the chair. He hadn't even noticed I'd left his side so I carefully slid the dusty old box out and opened it. In front of me was an awesome, if slightly rusty, battleaxe. It was similar to the Dragonbone – an axe from *Skyrim* – but it had a curved handle. And it was epic.

'Be careful, for Christ's sake!' Dar leapt to my side, plucked the axe from my hands and cradled it as if it were extremely dear to him.

'What is it, Dar?' I must have had sparks in my eyes because suddenly he was kneeling next to me, tenderly holding the axe for my appreciation.

'This is Snaghorn!'

Now Dar had sparks in his eyes too. The axe head looked like it could have been made from dragon bone, though obviously it couldn't have been! It was engraved with incredibly detailed carvings, like the Bayeux tapestry we'd been to see for our history trip last term.

'It must be so old. Is it yours, Dar?' I ran my fingers along the engravings on the handle. '*Kriger til Fred*. What does it mean?'

'Warriors until Peace.' Dar's voice became all whispery and soft. 'I haven't seen this for decades,' he said.

'I use an axe just like this one in *Skyrim*.' I carefully took the axe from Dar and held it up to the light.

'Skyrim? Is that some type of Chinese fighting style?'

'No, Dar, it's a game on my PS4.'

Dar seemed hideously unimpressed.

'No, Dar, it's awesome. You get to go anywhere you want and fight dragons and elves and orcs. And you have magic spells you can level up. It's an old game, like eight years old, but it's still awesome.'

Dar traced his hand along the shaft, rubbing away layers of dust to reveal yet more awesomeness.

'Such a clever design. A truly devastating weapon. Not just for show, you know.' Dar tapped the handle. 'The curvature. A devastating blow and a slice … No, like this.' Dar removed my second hand from the axe and helped me hold it single-handedly. 'The wonderful thing about an axe such as this, my little habbadehoy, is that it can be concealed. Under a cloak, or behind a shield … and then *swoosh*.' We chopped the air together.

'Did it cost much?' I seriously, totally, absolutely needed my own Snaghorn.

'It was gifted to me. Many, many years ago. By a great Nordic craftsman by the name of Egil Einer Oppegard.' I could see the pride in Dar's face as he cradled his treasure. 'The fighter from the farm who inspires terror.' Dar whispered, suddenly deep in his own thoughts.

'What? Who, Dar?'

'His name. Egil Einer Oppegard! It means the fighter from the farm who inspires terror. Huh, I haven't spoken that name for many, many decades.'

'You must have done something very special for a gift like this.'

Dar sighed and placed the axe gently back in its box, then pushed the box back into its cubbyhole.

'We do what we do,' Dar mumbled as he hobbled to the wheelchair.

I rushed to help, hit by a sudden realisation that I'd connected with my grandfather for possibly the first time ever.

'Come on, boy. Let's test out the off-road wheelchair.'

Dar had snapped out of his memories and our moment had gone.

Dar was pretty good at bribery, or emotional blackmail depending on which way you looked at it. He knew that after my soul-destroying lunch I'd crumble at the offer of a chow mein Pot Noodle and chocolate. I also found out later that Mum'd had a hand in the manipulation because I found her note in Nana's kitchen drawer while looking for batteries for William's LeapPad.

Ways to get Brandon off his butt and help out:

1) Use guilt!

2) 1 packet of MAOAMs = 1 medium chore.

3) His face WILL disintegrate if he doesn't clean his teeth.

4) He will pretty much do anything for £2.

5) If in doubt add a chow mein Pot Noodle.

6) If still not working, layer on more of (1).

Unfortunately, I realised too late that I'd been had again. Still, at least I'd be coming back from my kidnapping, hiking, hell mission with two pounds and a hot Pot Noodle to look forward to.

My twelve-year-old lungs were on fire. It was bad enough that the dust-filled shed had caused my allergies to flare, but now the cold afternoon air and biting wind were mocking me too; seeking out my bones in the most hideous manner. The wheelchair weighed a ton, and William, who'd come to meet us, was now sitting on Dar's lap and mocked my every word as I huffed and puffed across the rutted fields. This was not an epic day. What … so … ever.

I stopped for a well-needed rest and William ran off to find a big throwy stick to take back to Wrigley.

'Shhh.' Dar pointed to the hedge.

'What?' The cold air bit my tongue like an angry snake.

'It's a nuthatch.' Dar seemed excited.

I spotted the small bird shuffling up and down a tree, clicking its beak in and out of the bark.

'Incredible birds. And rare too!' he said, as if he'd sensed my interest fizzling away. 'I've seen one see off a kestrel before. That's a warrior if ever I saw one. One of the bravest birds there is.'

Fantastic. The great unwanted bird masterclass was rearing its ugly head again. I blew on my hands.

'So what does my name mean, Dar?' I said, trying to steer the conversation back to something more interesting.

'It means brave,' he replied.

I laughed at the irony. Me – bullied, wheezy, anxiety-wrecked. Named after the one thing I absolutely wasn't.

Dar called William back.

'My Dragonbone axe needs two hands to use, and I had to get the dragon-armour perk to create it. I needed three dragon bones, two ebony ingots and two leather strips. But yours isn't dragon bone, Dar. What's yours made from?'

Dar chose to ignore me, and I resumed pushing the ten-ton wheelchair across the soggy field. William clambered back onto Dar, pointing excitedly into the distance.

'Dar, the forest. Where the trolls live. Giddy-up, Bub!' William screeched as the wheels sank further into the mud. I didn't. I totally giddied down. 'Can we visit the trolls in the wood? Please?'

'Not today,' Dar replied, patting William on the knees to shush him. Then he adjusted his hearing aids and pulled his cap tight over his ears.

'If it isn't dragon bone, what is it made of?' I said, still struggling for breath as I pushed.

'But what about Forfaltrot? He might be starved hungry,' William said.

'So, maybe it is dragon bone then, Dar. Dar!'

But Dar only wanted to talk to William now. 'Shush, little bean. Remember the Kriger promise.'

William shrugged and grabbed Dar's cap, swinging it in the air as wisps of my grandfather's hair danced around in the breeze. Dar was not impressed.

'Kriger! Warrior until peace,' I declared, remembering what he'd said earlier.

'Can we, Dar? Can we? I promise to be quiet as a mouse.' William wasn't giving in and I could see Dar becoming more and more vexed as he snatched at the air, desperate to rescue his cap from William's lightning-fast hands.

'Not today, William!' Dar replied, wrestling his cap from my little brother's grip and forcing it back over his ears. The veins were beginning to raise in his neck and I wondered if his head might burst if he pulled his hat down any tighter.

'So, is a Kriger a real thing then, Dar? Were you a Kriger? And is that why you got given the battle axe?' I sped up and headed for the forest looming in the distance.

Dar fiddled with his hearing aids, no doubt desperate to turn them off.

'Not today, Brandon. It's getting late now.' He sounded irked.

The wind licked my cheeks as I ignored my grandfather and pushed on hard.

'You need to bring Snaghorn into my school and slice up *Aiden Hunt* with it. That'd make him think twice.'

'Trolls. Trolls. Come out and see me!' William screeched.

'Can I borrow it and use it around the farm? You know, chop some wood, throw it around a bit?' I imagined myself sneaking around the farm at night, chasing giant rats, swinging Snaghorn above my head, imagining I was a Dragonborn, level sixty-six.

'Brandon, turn back now please!'

Dar's words snapped me rudely out of my thoughts. Freezing tears streamed down my cheeks as I pushed on hard.

'Brandon, enough. I want to go home now.'

'Trolls. Trolls. We're going to see the trolls,' William sang, as I pushed harder, faster.

'Stop, Brandon. Turn back now!'

Running and pushing. Pushing and running.

Velociraptor veins pulsated at Dar's temples as he continued to fiddle with his hearing aids and the huge trees of the forest grew ever nearer.

'Can we feed them chocolate? Can we sing to them?' William screeched.

'Yeah, Dar. Do they eat chocolate and sweeties?' I mimicked.

Pushing and running. Running and pushing.

We were now just a hundred metres or so from the edge of Pitchbury Wood.

'Trolls, come out and see me!' William screeched.

Running and pushing. Pushing and running.

'Stop, Brandon. Stop! You don't know what you're doing!'

'Course I do. We're going to see some trolls, Dar. Real-life, kick-ass, living, breathing trolls!'

All of me hurt. From the laughing, from the pushing. The cold wind took hold of my guts but I ran as hard as I could. Faster. Harder. Closer.

'*Wheee.*' William shrieked.

'ONWARDS TO THE TROLLS!' My battle cry echoed through the trees as I imagined storming the dungeons in pursuit of the Gauldur Amulet, Snaghorn swinging as the enemies scattered around me – full of terror.

'Shut your damned mouth, boy! Do you want the entire world to know our business?' Dar roared.

But I just laughed and pushed on.

And then Dar exploded.

'DO AS YOU'RE TOLD, YOU DISOBEDIENT TOWN RAT ****!' Dar let rip with the proper, full-on F-word and grabbed my arm ferociously over his shoulder. It really hurt.

'You HORRIBLE, DISOBEDIENT, NASTY little children!'

The venom in his voice shocked me to my toes. I suddenly felt incredibly small and became rooted to the spot. Dar's ears slid back in full-on Jurassic mode. William began crying, my bottom lip went mental … and then there was quiet, except for my rasping breath, William's sniffles and the beat of my heart in my ears.

I knew every bad word but somehow, coming from Dar's mouth, it seemed even worse!

'Take me home.' Dar was breathless.

We headed back to the farm in silence.

We turned the corner of the yard and were confronted by a long fancy silver car in the driveway. It was the kind of car a top football manager might drive. Dar's face blanched as white as my new trainers and he lifted William carefully from his lap.

'Go bounce, little bean.'

William hugged Dar, then scurried around to the back of the house where the trampoline stood.

'I'll be there presently. See if you can touch the clouds today.'

When William was out of sight he wheeled himself slowly towards the car. I followed.

Dar sighed and kicked the tyre angrily, then exhaled deeply. He continued huffing, peppering his breath with hushed, feisty F-words.

Then he turned to me.

His expression was like mine when me and my mates do a Brainlicker or Toxic Waste challenge. I hoped Dar wasn't angry with me anymore but I couldn't tell.

'Please don't copy this, boy,' he said, fuming. 'But he is a villain of the highest order.' Then he grunted, sucked up the contents of his lungs from deep within, and spat onto the car.

'Who, Dar?' I asked, still shaken but curious all the same.

'Lackshaft! A very bad man indeed,' he replied.

In shared silence, we watched the revolting sputum slide down the car's windscreen. 'You must not, under any circumstances, mention anything about Pitchbury Wood.

Anything. Do you understand me? No, of course you don't. How could you? Just … just be polite and follow my lead.'

Dar was deathly serious, and I was not going to cross him anymore today.

Ever again actually, thinking about it.

'Okay, Dar. But can I please just ask one more thing?' Dar nodded. 'You don't really believe trolls exist, do you?'

Dar pulled off his cap and scratched at the few wispy hairs on top of his head.

'You just need to do as you're asked. And trust me. Can you do that, my little habbadehoy?'

Dar smiled up at me and I felt reassured. Confused, burning with a million questions, but reassured all the same.

'Yes, Dar. I understand.' I nodded hard to signify my total understanding, still stinging from his rage.

I began pushing him towards the house.

'Say absolutely nothing!' His tone was superhero cold.

He moved into his indoor wheelchair while I scraped the mud from my boots onto the heavy iron crocodile at the back door. Neither of us spoke. Then we entered the house.

I quickly wheeled Dar through, hearing the sound of muttering and clanking crockery.

I could sense his urgency. Something serious was clearly going down.

Dar composed himself for a moment, then lifted the heavy door latch to the lounge.

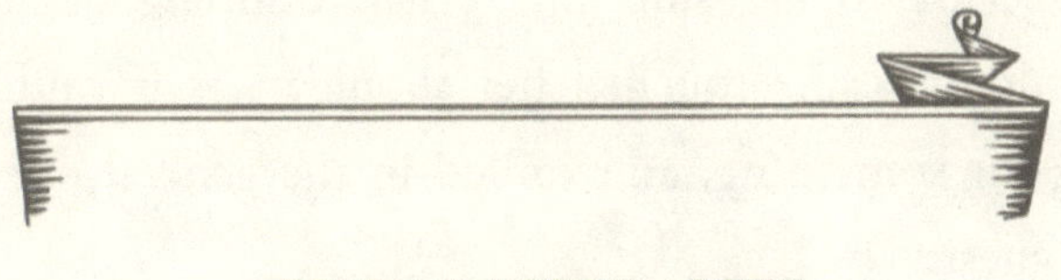

CHAPTER SIX

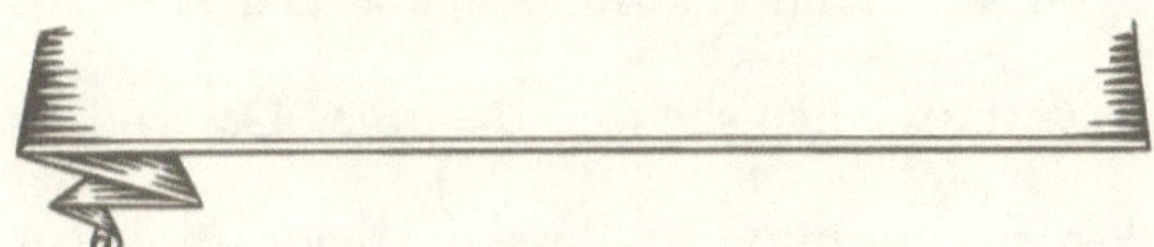

The Repugnant Guest

An old man rose to meet us. He was dressed immaculately. And fat. Not *just any kind of fat. A colossus. A jelly of a man. As he moved, every part of him undulated – like each ripple was applauding the one in front of it.*

'Basil, how lovely to see you.'

I saw the flex in Dar's jaw as he welcomed the guest. The guest took Dar's hand and shook it vigorously.

'Brandon, I'd like you to meet Councillor Basil Lackshaft.'

Dar was pretty good at pretending to be nice.

'Nice to meet you,' I said in my smartest voice, mirroring Dar's perfect manners. This was clearly the perfect opportunity to prove the maladjusted town rat knew how to mind his manners in public.

Nana Biddle held her gaze on us until Dar broke free and wheeled to her side. She began clapping her hands rhythmically as he touched her shoulder, as if cautiously feeling for something, and smiled in the general direction of the guest.

'Are you well, Hilde?' Basil looked at Dar as he spoke.

'She's with us when she feels the urge,' Dar said softly.

Lackshaft leant into Dar. 'I see the pylon's finally up. No more trouble from Tendring Council, then?'

There was something not right with this man. He spoke kindly, and with a mild Scottish accent, but his eyes said something totally different, like they were trying to hide under his eyebrows. Aayush – my second-best friend, trusted wing-man and elite sniper in *Fortnite* – called them paedo eyes: the eyes of a monster hiding beneath the skin of a man.

Dar shook his head, lowering his bottom lip. 'And for that I thank you ... again.' He smiled, though I got the feeling it had been forced.

Lackshaft took a gargantuan slurp of tea. 'Splendid. Because we can't have all the pylons mysteriously falling down willy-nilly.' He paused and stared in my direction. 'Can we, sonny?'

I shrugged. Like I gave a crap! I was too busy keeping an eye on William through the window and avoiding eye contact with Dar.

'We may be a wee crease on the edge of the map, but we do need our phone service.' Lackshaft replaced his cup and saucer on the table with a clatter. 'And electricity supply!'

He looked towards Nana Biddle, then over to Dar, and finally to me as I settled on the windowsill and pulled out my phone.

'And how did you say it happened again?' Lackshaft fixed his eyes on me as he questioned Dar. I didn't like those eyes one bit. Crocodile eyes. And I was the helpless turtle on my lily-pad windowsill.

Dar sighed and smiled at Nana Biddle as he took a KitKat from the silver tea tray. He slowly peeled off the paper wrapper and traced his fingernail across the metal foil.

'We've been through this, *Councillor*.' Dar snapped the biscuit fingers apart and reached into one of his many pockets. He pulled out a narrow blue book. 'Perhaps I could write you a cheque. Say, two hundred pounds for your charity. Saint Augustus Hospice, if I'm not mistaken.'

Lackshaft leant forwards and clasped his hands together.

'Put your chequebook away, David. We both know your bank account is as empty as your corn barn ... and your promises.' Lackshaft opened a black briefcase and lifted a large file onto his lap, then placed a tiny pair of glasses over his meatball nose. 'A gracious gesture indeed. But tell me, what good is a farmer who is in debt to the parish?' He ran his finger down a page in the folder, nodding slowly as he inspected the words. 'To the tune of several hundred thousand pounds. You have no livestock. No machinery worth its salt. No harvest. No income.'

The councillor leaned closer into Dar as if to make an important point.

'All you really have is an empty husk of land. You are no more a farmer than I am. Surviving on a meagre pension and subsidised by the district council. Sell the land, clear the debt and we can all go on our merry way.'

Dar took hold of the councillor's wrist. I could see the pressure in his whitening knuckles. His jaw flexed, and I heard his teeth grind.

'I won't sell.'

The councillor patted Dar's hand – the way Mrs Grimes, my geography teacher, did to my head when I hadn't done my homework. The incredibly patronising way.

Dar released his grip. Nana Biddle's piercing gaze was now firmly on Lackshaft.

I felt suddenly very uncomfortable. Stuck in the window bay with nowhere to hide, something ugly, some ugly adult thing, was panning out in front of me. And so, as you do in these situations, I turned to my phone and opened my chat app. Shane was online.

ME: *Watsup Tyrian?*

SHANE: *Pontins clubhouse. How's crapville?*

ME: *CRAP! Wish I was there!!!*

SHANE: *Me2 … wen u bak????????*

ME: *Nevr at dis rate* ☹

I glanced up at my grandfather. Lackshaft was leaning right in now, emphasising every word.

'You'll not intimidate me, *Farmer* Ballard. It's quite simple. Clear your debts and sign over your land to the parish or it will be taken from you under warrant before winter comes.'

'I don't know what you want from me!' Dar snapped. 'And for what. On what evidence?'

'I want the truth, Farmer Ballard! It's no mystery why I've lost four trucks and have men jumping ship left, right and centre.' Lackshaft sneered into Dar's face.

Dar's eyes narrowed. 'If you want to obtain a warrant via the proper channels and search my farm for whatever it is you think you know, then you feel free, *Councillor*.' Dar, although hunched up in his wheelchair, was pretty fierce when he wanted to be. 'Beyond that, I suggest you stay out of my business. And I'll stay out of yours.'

My phone alert chimed.

SHANE: *Havin fun?*

I lifted my eyes to the angry discussion, most definitely not having any fun at all.

ME: *Rather have piranhas eat my nutz. Horrible!*

SHANE: *Ahahaha. Soz.*

ME: *Can't you come over when you home?????*

SHANE: *Rather eat homeless man poop* ☺

<HUNTMASTER GENERAL HAS JOINED THE CHAT>

HUNTMASTER: *I'll come!*

SHANE: *Hi Aiden* ☺

My heart missed a beat. Aayush and *Aiden* were mates. Aayush must have added him to *our* group chat. Idiot! He knew he was my arch enemy – surely he should have been more loyal.

I could have asked Aayush to block him but that would have been pointless. I'd have had to be honest about the reasons but then I'd have looked like a bitch. *Aiden's* bitch! I could have been walking on the moon and he'd have still found a way to get inside my head, for God's sake.

ME: *What do you want Aiden?*

HUNTMASTER: *Just wanted to say hi.*

ME: *Yeah, well I'm talking to Shane.*

I slammed my phone down hard, probably as angry as Dar seemed to be right now. And now Dar's lip had curled, just like Wrigley's had the other day when I'd tried to take away his stick.

'You're so fixated with my land, *Councillor*. It's not healthy.' Dar looked across at me in the window bay. His eyes were filled with sadness, so I avoided them and waved to William, who bounced, without a care in the world, on the trampoline.

'Your land? Hah!' Lackshaft's voice had changed. It was lower, quieter, not nice at all. 'It ceased being your land when your father stood before the land committee half a century ago and swore under oath. And like you now, he expected us to buy his lies and continue to turn a blind eye.'

The councillor wrote a few notes on the page and stared hard at my grandfather. 'You'll pay your dues … or *we will* take the farm.'

A single tear rolled down Dar's cheek, navigating the furrows until it settled on his shirt collar.

'This is our home, Councillor.' His voice was suddenly very small.

PING!

My phone was becoming a good distraction – despite the moron on the other end.

HUNTMASTER: *Don't be like that. Just thought you'd like to know I had a lovely afternoon out with my dad.*

SHANE: *Don't Aiden … he's got it tough right now.*

My fist clenched, the knuckles turning from pink to red to white.

HUNTMASTER: *We saw The Meg … had Nandos. Was a right laugh I tell you.*

Aiden wanted me to bite and I wasn't giving it.

ME: *Shane, I'll call you later. On a phone.*

HUNTMASTER: *So much fun! Epic fun!!! Seen your dad lately????*

I looked over at Dar, but it was too much. I could tell that Nana Biddle was finding it difficult as she was rocking again. I was alone with my phone … and reminded myself it was just words. JUST WORDS. Hateful words from the ugly mouth of an evil moron.

ME: *Just p**s off Aiden. I don't care!*

It was easy being brave on a small screen, and while my language might seem a bit salty, It was necessary. *Aiden* is a freak. Captain of our year's rugby team and a spiteful bully. One of the worst. And there's no escaping him. To date, I'd had four nosebleeds, untold kicks to the nuts, a black eye, a split lip and a hideous Bunson burn.

HUNTMASTER: *Oh yeah, haven't got a dad have ya!*

SHANE: *Leave it out Aiden.*

<HUNTMASTER GENERAL is typing …>

HUNTMASTER: *Where's daddy gone???? Oh yeah … ditched your dumb lard of a mum for a proper one!!!!! Coz he's my dad now. Me and my good old dad. Off to Florida next week to have all the fun in the world. And you're stuck with the corpses while your mum's getting drunk!!!!*

<HUNTMASTER GENERAL has been blocked>

SHANE: *Sorry mate.*

ME: *Thanks* ☺

Sure, maybe they were only words, but they were sharp and cut all the way from my eyes to my heart. I knew it wasn't good to hate, but I hated him … probably too much. And my parents? Not my dad. It was Mum I had the problem with because she'd let him go. She'd let him leave and he ran right into the arms of Verity Hunt – *Aiden's* mum! So my hate was squarely with *Aiden* and today it hurt so much it took my breath away. I tucked my phone behind the photo frame on the windowsill.

Dar was probably right after all. Being constantly connected was no good thing. I grabbed the phone again and switched it off, then slid it back out of sight.

Lackshaft closed the file and returned it to his briefcase. The glasses went into their holder, then they too were put in the case.

'You want to keep your farm … and you still can, David. *If* you allow me to help you.'

Dar shook his head and sighed deeply.

'There's nothing to tell. The tractor broke the pylon. Pugwash wasn't paying attention and reversed into it. A simple farming accident. Nothing less, nothing more. And if your men crashed their trucks while trespassing on my land, it's nobody's fault but yours. Now, if you haven't got anything better to do with your time …' Dar stretched himself tall.

The councillor levered himself from the chair and approached my grandfather. 'Then you leave me no other option.'

He leant into Dar's personal space and placed his hands on each arm the wheelchair. Their eyes met – at war with each other.

'Give them up, David! Don't let pride destroy everything your ancestors worked so hard to provide for you … *Farmer Ballard*.'

At that moment, Dar seemed very old indeed.

'It's not pride. It's what's right. You've had your men scouring my farm for decades. Poking around, invading our privacy. And you've found what? Nothing! Whatever you think you know … you're mistaken.'

Lackshaft rose, straightened his tie and clapped his hands theatrically in Dar's face.

'Bravo. Forgive me for not calling for an encore. Righteousness never put bread on the table.' The fat councillor grabbed his briefcase and headed for the door. 'And it certainly won't keep a roof over your head. I'll see myself out.'

Hunched up small in the window bay, hoping I might

disappear, I watched the councillor's car speed off along the road. I wanted to kick myself hard, certain there was something I could have done or said to help. But I did nothing.

With my head low and tucked into my knees, I caught Nana Biddle embracing my grandfather out of the corner of my eye. I knew he was crying so turned to look outside and watched William on the trampoline instead.

Inside, I was crying too.

Part Two

The Reluctant Fart-Catcher

CHAPTER SEVEN

The Family Curse

I'd got used to 'sitting in' on Dar's bedtime stories. And by that, I mean crouching just out of sight in the hall. It made me feel not quite so alone. Mum and William would soon be leaving, and Dar was due to visit the hospital and have his cast cut off. I hoped he'd be less angry afterwards.

The verbal meltdown I'd triggered and the horrible confrontation with Councillor Lackshaft played on my mind. This evening, I added Dar to all my other daily worries. His voice sounded so tired.

'I promise,' said Dar. 'But it might have to wait until your next visit.'

William was wide-eyed, propped up high on his pillows. 'And will you hold my hand so I'm not so so scared?'

'You have my word, my little habbadehoy.'

'Where do the chickens come from?' William inched over to the edge of the bed and snuggled into Dar, gently rubbing my grandfather's hairy ear lobe between his fingers. Only a six-year-old could find comfort in that. There was probably more crap in Dar's ears than in the toolshed.

'So many questions, little bean. Remember the awful stink last week when the wind blew from the west? Well, that was Wally Morgan's farm – the chicken farm across the fields. And it smells far worse in the summer, I can assure you.'

William chuckled and held his nose. He didn't seem at all bothered by Dar's earlier outburst.

'Chickens die – many of them – long before they end up on a supper plate. And Wally Morgan scoops up the dead'uns and piles them on his muckheap behind the silos.'

'What's a silo?' William fished a booger from his nose and slipped it behind the headboard.

'It's a huge metal tower that holds all the chicken feed.'

'Si-low.'

'That's right. Clever boy.'

'Because I know all the Pokémon too.'

'I know! So once a month, I tiptoe over there in the dead of night' – Dar walked his fingers up Williams chest and tickled him under the chin – 'and *borrow* a barrowload of smelly old chickens … or two … and use them—'

'To feed the you know who!' William clapped his hands enthusiastically.

Dar paused and took a few sips of his *Adam's ale*, clinking the ice cubes around as he drank. I knew full well it wasn't water. In the daytime, before lunch, it might be the tap crap, but after noon it was always gin or vodka … or both.

'I'm sorry I shouted those words today, little bean.'

William nodded timidly.

'They were angry words. But I was only—'

'Phew, so you don't hate me then?' William whispered.

Dar was taken aback. 'Pifflebunk! You are quite the most marvellous little habbadehoy I know.'

William curled into Dar. He goes all squirmy like that when he gets too much praise … so it doesn't pay to go overboard.

'Are there stranger dangers in there? Inside the trees?'

Dar nodded. 'Maybe.'

'And you were protecting us … from dangers?'

'Possibly. But we keep all that to ourselves, right?' Dar sighed. The sound was long and gentle. 'I'm sorry I shouted at you, Brandon.'

It didn't bother me that Dar knew my resting place. I was just thankful for his forgiveness.

'That's okay, Dar. I'm sorry I didn't listen.'

'Would you care to sit in?'

'Uh-uh. I'm comfy. And my tablet's on charge here. But thank you.'

Dar settled William down and gently wrapped the blankets around him.

'Do you know of Mahatma Gandhi, Brandon?'

'Uh-huh,' I replied, leaning my head on the door frame and peeking inside the room.

'Well, Gandhi said that the weak can never forgive, that forgiveness is an attribute of the strong. Do you understand that? Course you do – you're sharp enough.'

'Thank you, Dar.' I shifted my bum a bit so I was sitting just inside the doorway.

'You've nothing to seek forgiveness for. Remember that.' Dar paused and cleared his throat. 'Remember that, Brandon. As you tread life's path.'

'I'll try.' My voice came out very small.

'I suppose you'd both like to know why I reacted so despicably earlier today.' Neither of us answered. 'Councillor Lackshaft likes to think he's some punkins. But he's not. He's one of the worst.'

I watched Dar keenly.

'He has power, you see.' He gritted his teeth and wheeled around the room for a moment, tipping his chair into a wheelie to emphasise his point. 'And power can be a terrible thing in the wrong hands. Lackshaft is possibly the worst type of villain there can be.'

Then he spun around so hard I thought he might tip over. 'Lackshaft and his kind have paid close attention to happenings on our land since long before I was born. When my own father farmed the land before me, and his father before him.'

I'd studied the large gold-framed portrait of my great grandfather last weekend when I was bored. It hung over the radiator in the front hall; the heat had crafted a million cracks into the picture. The man had been built strong just like Dar. In fact, they looked similar, but Dar's dad had sadder eyes, nesting under massive eyebrows.

'A man of some influence once confessed to witnessing *occurrences* on our land. And ever since, there's been an invisible black mark against our family name.' Dar's voice had an edge of sadness. 'And that little mark carries hateful attention.'

William curled up, on the brink of sleep. 'Do you understand what I'm trying to tell you, Brandon?'

Although he was being rather cryptic, I thought I knew what he was trying to tell me.

'You mean trolls, don't you, Dar?'

'Yes, son. I do.'

Dar stared at me and I could see truth in his eyes.

'But, Dar, if – and that's a monstrous if – there are trolls living in the forest, why does that mean you could lose the farm?'

'It doesn't,' Dar replied. The life seemed to fizzle from his eyes. 'I could give them up tomorrow, betray them and hand them over to *Lackshaft* and his people. And that would be that. I'd probably even get a sizeable reward for my trouble. But I won't do that. I'd be a fiend!'

'But how can it be real? This is the real world, Dar. We're not in some fairy story with werewolves and sparkly vampires.'

Dar chuckled; some kind of mockery towards my point.

'What's so funny?' I wasn't buying it. I knew what was real! 'You really believe there are trolls in Pitchbury Wood, don't you?' I stared hard at Dar.

'The question isn't whether we believe, Brandon, but what we choose to do with the information. Were it true!'

'So,' I said, deciding to humour him, 'there are trolls in the forest, and that has something to do with Councillor Lackshaft, yeah?'

Dar nodded. A very serious nod indeed.

'And you're scared he's going to take the farm away. Why?'

Dar wheeled into the hall and gently closed William's door.

'Can I trust you, Brandon?' He looked down at me and raised his eyebrows. 'Can I trust you with possibly the most spectacular secret in all the world?'

I nodded hard as Dar held up his hand, as if to swear an oath like they do on Judge Rinder.

'You spit …' Dar gobbed on his hand and held it towards me. Totally gross but I did the same. 'And you shake.' We placed our hands together. 'I believe that modern people are over-informed. The Internets, around-the-clock news, newspapers, magazines … huh, you even get video news on your handheld telephone … from right across the world.' Dar counted out his thoughts on his fingertips – like a woodpecker … or a factpecker!

'I believe that all that news, all that knowledge, leaves gaps. Magical gaps where truths far too spectacular to comprehend reside. Everybody knows everything these days. Our heads are full of facts and information, passwords, numbers … all these vital things that must be learned and remembered. But really, we know nothing. Except what we are required to know.'

I was curious to see where this was going. 'So, you're saying the modern world is stupid? I know most of my teachers are.'

'Nope. Just overloaded with the stuff that doesn't matter. Man-made irrelevance. A form of subterfuge, like a magician's sleight of hand.'

I was both confused and intrigued by Dar's wisdom. Then I got it.

'So … we think we know everything while the really important stuff stays comfortably tucked away.'

'Exactly. Lackshaft and his ilk are responsible for keeping things simple. Making sure we continue to know what we know … and nothing more. Ponder it! What would happen if folk knew there were trolls galivanting around the forest? What do you think would happen?'

'I don't know, Dar. Last I heard, trolls weren't real. They'd probably be zapped, trapped or chopped up, or chucked in a monster zoo or freakshow or something.'

Dar placed his hand on my shoulder and rubbed it reassuringly. 'Or a fate so very much worse.' Then he rolled his creaky wheelchair across the hall. 'Oh, Brandon. It's hard to grasp, I know. So I suppose I'm just going to have to prove it to you, aren't I?'

He stopped in front of the door to his room.

'And, Brandon …'

'Yes, Dar.'

'You did well today, but there's one more job to be jobbed. And this one's a little more' – he checked there was no one around – 'exciting! You clearly need some answers. I get that. But you need to understand that if you discover something more than just the demented ramblings of an old man, you'll bear the responsibility of complete and total integrity. There must be absolute trust. Are we clear?' Dar raised his eyebrows and leaned forward. 'This could make your life incredibly dangerous. I'm not a young man anymore, and one day … well …' Dar sighed and patted my shoulder. 'It comes to us all, my little habbadehoy.'

I stared at him, searching for truth, madness, mischief … whatever. But all I saw was honesty and love.

He lowered his voice to a whisper. '*Kriger til Fred.* Are you ready to discover the truth?'

I nodded softly. I did need to know. Because something was different here on the farm, and Dar was totally, absolutely, firm in his beliefs. I had to get to the bottom of it. How could I not?

'Set your alarm for midnight. It's time to learn a secret or two!'

And with that, I was left alone.

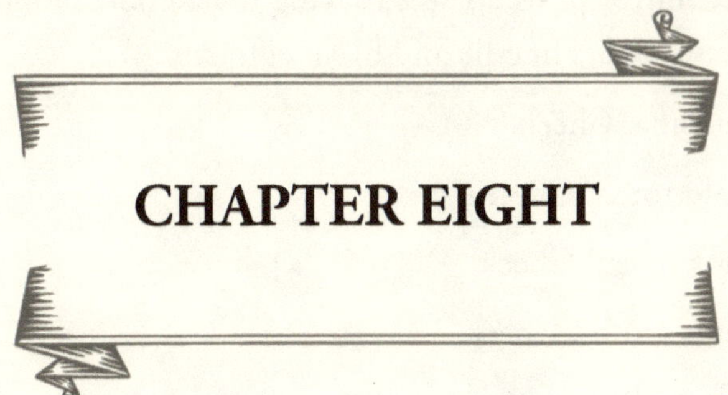

CHAPTER EIGHT

500 cc's of Adrenaline

The alarm on my tablet rang. It was midnight. Perhaps Dar had expected me to be tucked up in bed, but I'd just finished playing a series of very laggy games of *Clash Royale* with Aayush and Shane. So flipping annoying because my new tablet had the latest Nvidia graphics card and maxed-out RAM. The *Toxic Slab* was the envy of my friends. I'd spent the best part of three weeks clearing out Mrs Brightwell's back garden to save up for it. Proper hard summer graft. I named it after the bright green cover I bought to protect the gleaming aluminium case; because I'd smashed the screen of my last tablet in less than three months. And there was no way I'd let this little beauty fall to the same fate! The *Toxic Slab* really was the stuff of dreams. But here in the land of 3G it might as well have been a supersonic nuclear battle tank that fired buns and jellies. I was a laggy laughing stock.

Dar rapped lightly on the door: 12.02 a.m.

The mirror proved I was rocking the commando look – zip-up Star Wars hoodie and black combats.

Bandana. Check.

Head torch. Check.

Spy camera. Check.

Ninja gloves. Check.

Attack alarm. Check.

Thick socks so the wellies didn't chafe. Check.

It was on, like *Donkey Kong*.

I helped Dar hop across the yard. The wheelchair was far too conspicuous so we'd decided that now was the time to test the hiking crutches Mum had picked up from Dr Saunders. My shoulder helped Dar keep his balance as the crutches *tap-tap-tapped* on the concrete, providing the rhythm as we snuck through the shadows towards the timber shed.

Dar pulled a bird-crap-covered sheet from over a large green quad-bike. Then we wheeled it backwards and out of shed – gently so we didn't scrape the paintwork on the wall.

'You steer, Brandon.' He had that glint in his eyes. 'And I'll do the brakes.'

Dar locked the shed and I climbed between him and the handlebars on the quad. 'Tuck your legs in tight so I can reach the gears.' Dar showed me the red thumb stick that handled the acceleration. 'Nice and gentle or we'll end up in the ditch. Like this ...'

The quad eased forward, and we were on the move.

It was dark but the headlight showed us the way down the long mud track. Dar swapped his hand for mine and then I was driving. It was bumpy and mud-splattered and seriously cool – me and Dar riding out together on a risky late-night mission.

When we reached the top field, Dar changed gear and we really began to shift. There were rabbits everywhere! A hare sped across the treeline, chased by a fox. Then, to blitz that, a muntjac deer did a Mario jump right over a tall gate.

It was bitterly cold, but that didn't bother me.

'It's about a mile to the chicken farm.' Dar leaned into my ear as he spoke. 'We'll cling to the shadow of the hedgerows, keeping in a low gear … to keep the revs down.' Dar had already warned me that anything over half-throttle made the engine roar like a wild monster … and we most certainly didn't want to get caught. 'This, what we're doing tonight, Brandon, is tantamount to poaching! Like the boy and his father in *Danny, The Champion of the World*.'

Dar was gobsmacked to learn I'd never heard of it and promised to buy me a copy next time he visited Townsend's bookshop in Manningtree.

As we whizzed along the treeline, I imagined what it might be like to get caught by SWAT: tasered, lined up with my grandfather, bright lights shining in our eyes while we were forced to confess our crimes. I hoped kid poachers were treated leniently. Maybe I'd poke the finger at Dar!

By the time we pulled the quad over behind the long barn at the back of Wally's farm, I was a nervous wreck. In my mind, we'd spent three years in prison and I was no longer as innocent as when we'd started out.

'And there's definitely no cameras?' My voice came out a bit bleaty.

Dar was twinkling, clearly a braver man than me. 'Let's hope not!'

We hugged the shadows around the barn and I was sure we were close – the smell of rotten chickens was the worst gross ever. Was there a word for it? *Guffskudge.* There … now there was! It was the worst guffskudge my nostrils had ever encountered. I was glad I hadn't been eating much lately because I'd pretty sure I'd have vommed up a steaming puddle of spew.

The silo loomed in front of us. It looked like the Loony Toons tower from the old cartoons I watched with William. Several large rats scurried away as we reached the muckheap: a mountain of stench and runny filth. I was glad for my wellies, while my ninja scarf became a highly usable guffskudge mask. We put on our petrol-station gloves and dragged about fifty dead chickens into our bin bags. It was the most revolting experience ever but a good trade-off for the quad-bike ride.

As we snuck away from the muckheap, I spotted the hugest rat in the world. It was dragging the corpse of a fat rooster from the heap. It was probably almost the same size as the rooster too … a horrifically terrifying creature indeed.

Then I spotted half a brick on the floor. And then, our situation became bad. *Very very* bad!

In a flash, I grabbed the brick and launched it towards the rat. Not my greatest shot – the brick missed the rat and smashed into the metal silo. Then, like a mighty clap of thunder, a sonic boom filled the air.

We froze.

Dogs began barking, lights came on, and all hell broke loose.

'Run!' Dar shouted.

So we ran!

Dar grabbed my shoulder, working his crutch on the concrete like a piston: *tap-tap-tap*. Doors began slamming, claws scraped on concrete as dogs hurtled towards us, barking furiously. I'm sure I even heard a wave of police sirens and tank tracks on the streets.

Now we were outlaws.

We ran and ran and ran. The chicken sacks were flung onto the quad-bike trailer. Dar grabbed my hoodie and hauled me in there with them. The engine roared to life …

And we were off.

The engine screamed as we hurtled forward, and I fell back, only just stopping myself from falling out as my hands grabbed the sides of the trailer.

SHIT! There was a man with a gun.

Several large dogs gnashing at the fence.

A fat lady flapping around in her dressing gown.

Two huge teenage boys yelling into the darkness.

Were there blue lights flashing in the distance? Surely not already. But why not? *We'd committed a crime!*

Mud began to fly around us.

'Hold on, Brandon. You've gotta hold on tight!' Dar steadied his cap with one hand and motored the quad-bike forward with the other. The trailer was bouncing so hard that my eyeballs felt like they might flip upside down in their sockets. My tailbone bashed against the wooden floor … but all that mattered was not falling out.

Do not fall out. DO NOT FALL OUT.

Brambles and branches whipped my face as the world whizzed by.

Hold on tight. DON'T FALL OUT!

'Hang in there, Brandon. We're nearly home!' Dar screamed into the wind.

And I *was* hanging in there … for my life. I could see the farm in the distance and was sure the SWAT team would be on our tails by now. The speck of light from Dar's bedroom window was getting bigger and bigger.

Maybe we'd get out of this alive, after all.

We were going soooo fast! We even lifted off the ground from time to time. Every bump, every furrow left me rattled, cut and bruised.

Bang … the back of my head hit the trailer.

Crash … my tailbone and ribs battered.

Smash … I bit my tongue.

Faster. Stupidly fast. Closer to home … Closer to certain death.

The trees flew past in a blur. *Whoosh. Whoosh.* I was scraped, lanced, whipped by branches.

A shower of mud and glory – two badass chicken rustlers in the heat of battle. Rooster fugitives. *Oh God, I hope we get out of this alive!*

I was terrified. Exhilarated! And felt very much alive!

We slid around the corner at the end of the track. And kept on slipping. Like we were on ice. A massive metal beast out of control.

And then we slid, in bullet time … towards the new ditch that Pugwash had dug last month to take care of the heavy autumn rain. The quad careered over the edge, moon-like gravity taking control as we plunged upside down towards its murky depths.

I felt a sharp pain … then nothing.

CHAPTER NINE

The Dark of the Other Side

I force open my eyes. A sharp pain in my legs drives hot sick into the back of my throat and my heartbeat thumps in my chest like a sledgehammer. Everything is black. The air is thick with the reek of petrol. Chest deep in water, I scramble backwards with my arms, clawing at my bedroom floor. Terrified. Confused. Why is it so muddy? I can't see my bed and just want to go back to sleep.

Nothing makes sense!

The bedroom floor is awash with muddy water. All my furniture is smashed to smithereens. Where are the shelves with my neat row of pop-heads? All my stuff? And what about Lil? She can't swim … can she? Cats hate water.

'Mum.' I look around, thrashing frantically in the thick water like a crocodile. 'MUM, WHERE ARE YOU?'

Normal noise doesn't exist. There's just a rush of whistling amid the destruction and chaos. Dad put those shelves up … and now they're all smashed. The faint glow of my bedside light catches my eye. I splash towards it, fighting against the tide, and grab the lamp. My body is suddenly gripped by a sinking feeling of despair as anxiety grips my spine. Why is the lamp attached to the front of a quad-bike? That's not right. That's not possible.

'MUM!'

And then, with a burst of light and the crashing waves of a mighty ocean, my bedroom walls slipped away and my mind returned to the ditch.

Oh shit.

My hands swiped at the smashed lamp, feverishly wiping away dirt and mud. I yelped as a sliver of glass punctured my palm. But now I could see. The nightmare has passed but now I was faced with a reality so much more terrifying. We'd been in an accident and I needed to get my crap together. *Come on Brandon. Do it. Now!*

The quad was upside down in the ditch. The trailer was smashed up in the hedge and petrol was spilling everywhere from a gash in the side of the fuel tank. But where was Dar? I rolled around in the water like a crocodile in a death roll, feeling around for my grandfather. My heartbeat thumped hard and fast in my ears. The pain in my leg was almost unbearable. I staggered to my knees, hoisting myself up with the quad-bike axle.

'Help!' I roared into the dense silence of the night. And then I saw Dar, his legs buckled by the edge of the ditch, body stuck behind the quad. Trapped! I pulled myself around to him, tears streaming down my face … and not just because of the pain.

The upside-down quad was on top of him, pinning his torso under the oily water. I dragged myself up onto my feet and grabbed the heavy metal frame with both hands, lifting for all my worth. It didn't budge. I strained again, so hard that something clicked in my back, forcing a scream from my tired, aching lungs. A proper all-out scream-for-Mum pain. I took a huge breath and slipped under the water.

I found Dar's hand. Gave it a squeeze. He didn't squeeze back. *Come on, Dar. Don't do this to me.* I used my free hand to feel my way to his face. My mouth found his, and his head moved towards mine.

I blew my air into him.

His hand squeezed.

Oh, thank God. He's not dead.

I tried to break my hand free but he wouldn't let go. I lifted my face above the water and took an almighty breath then ducked down into the cold and passed it onto Dar. We couldn't keep this up. We'd die from hypothermia – like those poor people on the news from Somalia in their rubber boats. My mind was racing. I forced one last breath into Dar and broke free from his grip.

I climbed onto the bottom of the quad-bike and made myself as tall as I could. I could just see the track above the ditch. The light from the farmhouse felt like a distant planet.

'HELP.'

My brain formed the words but I'm certain my mouth just roared the language of terror. 'HELP. Somebody help us. Please!'

I scrambled back down into the ditch and fell, knocking my chin on the frame and slipping back into the freezing water.

It was no good. Too cold. So terribly cold.

'Please somebody … *please help*.' My little voice returned. I slipped under the water but couldn't find Dar's hand.

I closed my eyes … just for a second … just for a break. So cold.

Then I was flying! Dar, me, the quad-bike, all soaring through the air together. I wasn't scared, not anymore. Neither was I cold. This was just a magnificent dream in which we were free from our watery tomb. Not in the ditch, Not in my bedroom. Nowhere in particular. We just *were*.

I forced my eyes open, squinting through muddied lids, and just made out a colossal figure. I looked to my side. A vast hand clutched the back of Dar's coat, carrying him. I looked down and saw that I was being carried too. We moved across the farm like the wind. I stretched my neck, trying to see more, but the pain advised against it; so I just closed my eyes and slipped into unconsciousness, my drifting mind trying to make sense of the impossible.

CHAPTER TEN

A New World Order

I was covered in straw. High up. Very high up. The wind whipped and slapped me to my senses. I could see the farmhouse below, and the grain pit and the stables. I crawled to the edge of the makeshift bed and tried to work out the facts. I was on top of a huge straw stack, maybe a hundred feet up.

How the hell had I even got up here? But more importantly … where was Dar?

My head pounded. I felt my forehead, wincing as I located a painful lump. And with it came a rising wave of anxiety, washing over me like a tsunami. First a tingle in my toes, then rising horrifically up my body. Then came the aftershocks – clammy hands, pounding heart, dry mouth and that dizzy, sinking feeling of utter despair.

It's just adrenaline. Only adrenaline! I told myself over and over as the numbness set in and I withdrew into myself. I checked my pockets for the Rescue Remedy but it wasn't there. Damn!

It's just adrenaline. It will pass. I remembered my counsellor's explanation of the fight-or-flight mechanism and took a moment to compose myself, pulling my jumper over my face to help regulate my breathing. The terror began to subside. *Let it pass. It's nothing you haven't got through before*, I reminded myself, imagining Dr Tizzard, my counsellor, by my side.

My breathing settled. I was able to focus. I looked around and spotted Dar's sleeve poking out from a nest of straw next to where I'd been sleeping. I rushed over and knelt by his side, terrified of what I might discover.

I pulled all the straw to the side, uncovering the top of his body. There was no blood, no damage I could see, but he was still. Too still. I rested my ear by his mouth … and heard his breathing. Soft. Weak.

Yes! Dar was alive.

His head was filthy, caked in dried mud, but there was a clean strip right across the middle of his face covered in goo. It stunk of rotten egg.

'Dar, can you hear me?'

I took hold of his hand and gave it a light squeeze.

'Talk to me, Dar. Can you talk to me? Please.'

His body shifted slightly, and I scraped away the straw that was covering his legs. They seemed okay, but the material of his trousers was ripped.

'Please talk to me, Dar. DAR! Can you move your legs?'

He groaned weakly, and his legs replied, lightly bending at the knees. The leg with the ripped trouser leg was covered in dried mud, thought this looked like it had been added – like the swallows' nests high up on the roof of the farmhouse.

All in all, we both seemed to be in decent shape.

My mind raced as I lowered myself down the wooden ladder running down the side of the straw stack. What the hell had happened and how had we got so up high?

It wasn't properly light yet – just that cold blue twilight before the sunlight warms up the atmosphere. My watch screen was cracked from the accident, but it read six-fifteen.

I ran around the wood shed and along the muddy track until I reach the accident site. The shattered trailer decorated the hedgerows like a Christmas tree and there was a massive tear in the earth where we'd hit the ditch. Below that was a large crater … but no quad-bike. I stood there for a moment, trying to visualise what had happened, but between being in the ditch and waking up in the straw there was nothing.

Then I noticed the gaping hole in the hedge.

I ran to the end of the track and, sure enough, there were the deep furrows where we'd skidded to our terrible halt. I ran through the open gate and around the other side of the hedge.

And found the quad.

Upside down, easily a five-a-side football-pitch length across the field. I walked across, my brain desperately trying to draw a line between the dots. I crouched down to inspect the mangled wreck. It lay at the end of a twenty-foot trench, like it had been powered there with great force. The quad bike lined up perfectly with the gap in the hedge. Surely the crash wouldn't have caused this much damage, though. I looked at the gulley it had left. It was deep, like the trail from an incoming meteorite.

It didn't make sense. The metal seemed to have been ripped … no, pierced. Yeah, and in five places. Deep … the kind of holes you might find on a bowling ball. There was blood and matted fur wedged into one of the holes … like the stuff I'd found on the chicken fence. And it smelled of egg!

And then, while thinking myself ridiculous for even daring to consider the possibility, I worked it out.

We'd been rescued by a troll! A Herculean troll who could cannon a quad-bike halfway across a field, further than I could chuck a tennis ball with my left arm.

I ran back to the straw stack as fast as my legs would allow, my mind reeling.

By 7.15 a.m. we were bathed, dressed and sitting at the wonky kitchen table, drinking hot, sweet, tea.

Mum brought Nana and William in for breakfast.

'Sleep well?' Mum fought her mop of curly hair into a messy ponytail.

Dar nodded enthusiastically. I tried to get my own head working but it refused. My body was numb but my brain was in turbo mode.

'What plans you got for today then, men?' Mum smiled, oblivious of our crazy night of terror.

I stared at Dar.

'Thought I'd take this little habbadehoy pike fishing.'

'Fishing! Yay!' William squealed.

'Not today, William. Today's Brandon's turn.'

Dar leaned across the table and planted turbo kisses on William's cheek. His voice sounded weak; I couldn't imagine what mine would be like if I found it.

I doubted that William knew he and Mum were going home today and that I was to be left here alone. Left here! The thought had passed my mind a thousand times since the moment I'd packed my bag at home. The sense of dread had made my stomach lurch on many occasions. But not today. Today, my stomach was churning to a different rhythm. A troll's rhythm!

'I'm sorry, little bean, but I'm taking Brandon to a very dangerous spot by the weir. To catch bitey fish. Another day,

I promise.'

William was clearly disappointed but soon tucked in to his Rainbow Drops and honey milk.

Trolls! It seemed ridiculous, and yet …

Trolls did not exist. Trolls could exist! Trolls did exist! Trolls were real! My head was like a washing machine, churning the ludicrous and the impossible back and forth.

Bigfoot. That could be a troll. People had spent their lives searching for it.

And the Loch Ness monster.

Aliens at Area 51.

God. New planets, solar systems. What else?

A while back, I'd read about loads of new sea creatures discovered in the depths of the ocean. Fascinating stories of what could be hiding in the bottom of the Mariana Trench, ten thousand metres under the sea. So why not trolls? I sneaked a couple of hits of Rescue Remedy, just to slow things down a bit.

Dar seemed way too cool with everything. But then, he knew! We'd crashed. Fact. And we'd been carried to safety by *something*. Fact. Something unexplainable. Fact. I hit the Rescue Remedy again and my brain gifted me a headache.

Dar squinted as he hugged my little brother. He was clearly in pain but gave nothing away.

Amid the anxiety and the headache, excitement coursed through my veins. The discombobulation of last night was filling me with something new and unfamiliar. And it felt great. Not one single word would spill from my lips to risk giving the game away. The thought that this heart-pounding, life-risking, fantastical adventure might come to an abrupt halt was beyond my comprehension.

And so, over breakfast, the morning after being saved by a troll, I found myself on a rollercoaster, like the one at Southend seafront, when Mum had to get the operator to let me off before it even moved. Like that … but this time, I didn't want to get off!

And the Southend rollercoaster incident … well … that didn't happen as long ago as you might think.

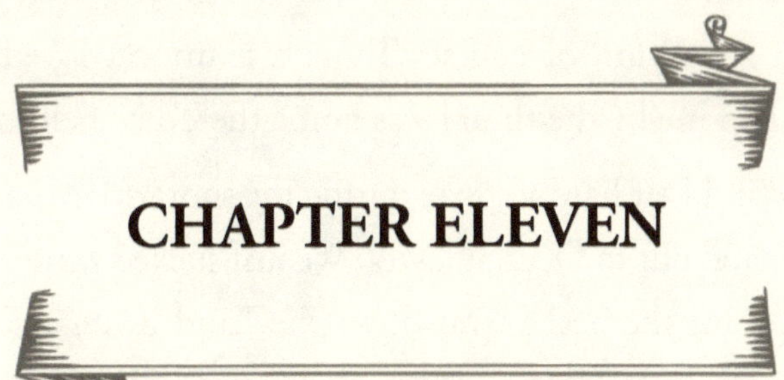

CHAPTER ELEVEN

The Truth and the Lure

I said my goodbyes, hugging Mum tightly though still severely angry with her for leaving. She seemed genuinely sad to leave me.

'Help out the best you can …'

'I wish you didn't have to go, Mum.' I was pretty surprised I wasn't hanging off her legs, begging to go home too. But things had changed.

'Your brother's back at school tomorrow. And, besides, you and Dar are besties now, right?' Mum kissed me on the forehead. 'He won't need your muscles much longer. You're getting stronger by the day, aren't you, Dad? And the work's almost caught up.'

I took in Mum's smell so it might rub off and stay with me for the next week. 'Chin up, Captain. You'll be home before you know it.'

William pressed his face against the car window as they left, watching all the way down the lane as we waved them off. I'd miss him, of course. Though if my cat loved him more than me by the time I was home there'd be hell to pay!

Me and Dar hardly spoke during the short drive to Lamb Corner and out to Dedham Mill. We just sucked wine gums, thankful for the peace. Dar drove the Land Rover right up next to the river. We'd had enough exercise to last the week, so there was no need to overdo it now.

He cut the engine and nodded slowly.

'It's time.' His voice was ice-cold and my heart skipped a beat, sensing it was time for some life-altering affirmations. 'Do you want to go first or shall I?' His expression was serious and I knew my take on the world was about to change forever.

'Last night we were saved by a troll.' I spat the words out and let them hang there. 'We had a terrible crash and you almost died. You would have … had we not been rescued' – I took a deep breath – 'by a troll.'

Dar raised his eyebrows, and I mimicked him.

'Could you describe it?' he said calmly.

OM*G, this was one mental conversation!

'I'm not really up on my trolls right now, Dar. Did you not hear me? We were rescued by a troll!'

Dar unscrewed his flask and poured hot sweet coffee into two little plastic cups.

'Was it big or small?' Dar blew on his drink and took a sip.

'It was a troll, Dar. A freaking troll. Big! The size of a tractor.' This was utterly surreal.

'Did it have chin hair?' Dar tugged at his straggly grey beard. 'Or a flat face, with one eye not quite perpendicular with the other? Did it snarl?'

I stared at my grandfather like he was suddenly broken.

'Does it matter, Dar? A troll came out of the night and threw your quad-bike like it was a ping-pong ball. A ping-pong ball, Dar! Shot it through the hedge … and it landed in the field by the water trough. A troll, Dar!'

Dar thought deeply about this and I just stared at him, mouth agape. I must have looked like a cartoon character.

'The quad-bike must weigh a few hundred weight and it's at least sixty yards to the trough. And you didn't see any distinguishing features?' Dar did some calculations with his fingers.

'Dar, we were half-dead! It was just one huge troll all around us. It held us in its grip like the Deathclaw in *Fallout*.'

'Deathclaw? That sounds fierce.'

'It's a huge dinosaur-lizard thing in a game we all play. They're kick-ass creatures. Well, I thought they were. Now I'm not so sure.' I sat up tall in my seat and slapped my cheeks – checking I was awake. 'Damn, Dar! *Trolls are real!*

My grandfather continued sipping his coffee. One blow, one sip. One blow, one sip. One blow, one sip.

'Dar, there are trolls in this world! Do you not compute how enormously, fantastically bonkers that is?'

This was crazy. We were sitting in a Land Rover, having a little troll chat over coffee. Like it was the most normal thing in the world.

'I thought it might have been Hodefisk but there's no way he could pitch the quad that far. He's just a babe. It was Forfaltrot. Had to be. Hodefisk struggles to break a birch tree, let alone a pylon.'

'Hodefisk? Forfaltrot? There's more than one?' I yelped, wanting to pinch myself back to reality. 'Do you remember what happened, Dar?'

He nodded. 'Though I wish I didn't.' He placed his arm around my shoulder. 'And I know I'd be dead had it not been for you.'

I hung my head in shame. 'I couldn't do anything,' My bottom lip went; I had no control over it. 'I couldn't stop the crash, couldn't lift the quad, couldn't …'

Dar hugged me hard.

'When your hand found mine under the water, Brandon, it was quite the most reassuring moment of my life. And then you gave me air. How on earth did you learn to do that?'

I shrugged. 'Off the telly.'

'Then maybe the idiot box isn't so terrible after all,' Dar said.

We hugged for a moment longer, then Dar leaned right into my ear and whispered, 'So now you know, my little habbadehoy. There are trolls in Pitchbury Wood.'

He smiled lovingly at me.

'And if it hadn't been for Forfaltrot, we'd both be dead,' I reminded him, hoping my bottom lip would sort itself soon. 'It—'

'He.'

'*He* must have heard me screaming. Good old troll.' For once, I was glad of my screechy, pre-pubescent voice.

'So … now that you've seen him with your own two eyes, what do you intend to do about it?'

I thought very hard for a second.

'Is this what it means to be a Kriger, Dar?' My eyes searched his as he nodded seriously.

Right there, right then, I decided to accept that trolls were real. How could I not? But there was still so much I needed to understand. Just to get my head around the enormity of the discovery.

'Ponder this, my little habbadehoy. *Let bravery be thy choice.* Recognise the truth. Being a Kriger is the ultimate truth. Doing what's right as opposed to what's easy. Do you understand?'

I didn't know what to think or understand at that moment. I probably couldn't have spelled my own name. So I just shrugged.

'So, yes, Brandon, this is what it means to be a Kriger. We forsake our own needs to protect those who cannot protect themselves. As we protect the trollfolk, the trollfolk protect us.'

'Then I think we should finish the mission, Dar.' My hand found my grandfather's. 'They deserve their chicken feast now more than ever.'

'And that, my dear boy, sounds like a plan, Stan.' Dar said, copying my saying – badly. 'I think we should extend it to a bushel of apples too. Seeing as it was hunger that brought them into the open. And you're fine with this? And most importantly, can keep it between ourselves.'

I nodded my hardest nod.

'Good.' Dar rubbed my shoulder. 'But first we catch supper!'

I suppose I should have been more surprised by Dar's confirmation; the world as I'd known it no longer existed. Yet that was absolutely fine by me. I'd hated that world. It was full of anger and rage and war and uncertainty. So if protecting trolls was Dar's mission, so much so that he was prepared to risk his farm and his life, that made it my mission too. *For the clan* – that was my gaming mantra with Shane and Aayush. (It used to be *To infinity and beyond* ... but we're not kids anymore.) It was the only thing that mattered. *Clan for clan*!

I was born to keep these kinds of secrets. And as mental and impossible and logic-defying as this was, I was ready to step up and be a Kriger.

The mill pool was a big water bowl, and this time of year it was as clear as Dar's gin. You could see all the tangled lily stems on the gravel bottom and occasionally a shoal of micro fish would dart by. Minnows, Dar informed me. One of the smallest fish in the river, alongside gudgeon and dace. The weir was closed today, barely more than a trickle of water seeping over the slimy green concrete platform.

'In full flow it can easily drag a grown man to his death,' Dar said. And then he went quiet for a bit, probably remembering the horrors of the previous night.

'Do you think you should go to the hospital, Dar?'

'Absolutely not,' he snapped. 'I'll ask Dr Saunders to check me over this afternoon.' He'd probably seen far too much of hospitals lately, and besides, farmers weren't the *hospitally* kind.

'But what about the—'

'Later, boy. First, we fish. We've both had a bit too much excitement for one night, and situations like this require a period of calm. So one can take stock.'

He tied a long metal trace onto the end of the fishing line with what he called a knotless knot.

'And there's nothing like a spot of fishing to quieten the soul.'

He twisted the line around itself about ten times, then tucked the end back through itself. 'Pike have teeth like razors. A fearless and voracious predator indeed.' He spat on the line and then pulled it tight with his fingernails. 'But he won't bite through a wire trace. That's the secret, Brandon.' He tugged the wire tight. 'Preparation is everything.'

He opened his tackle box and I was presented with almost a hundred colourful choices of fishing lure.

'This is a surface popper.' He pointed at a fat lure that looked like a dolphin. 'And that's a spinner,' he said, when I picked up the gold metal leaf with three deadly looking hooks hanging from the end. 'The pike will be lazy now, hiding under the weeds, poised to attack. How about we use this one?'

He pulled out a torpedo-shaped lure that had a jelly rubber tail. But I already had my heart set on the rubber frog!

We took turns casting.

'Dar?'

'Yes, my little habbadehoy.'

'Was the broken chicken fence anything to do with trolls?'

I flicked the rod across the mill pond. It was tricky getting the timing right but, with Dar's help, after a few attempts I managed to drop the frog just inches away from the overhanging elderberry tree every time.

'Yes, it was. And the pylon.' He nodded while demonstrating how to jerk the rod tip and regulate how fast I was reeling in. 'Count it out, Brandon.'

'One elephant, two elephant, three … four … five.'

'Allow the frog to sink just enough and then jerk the line.' Dar guided my hand to flick the rod in twitchy movements. 'That's it. Bit by bit … let 'em think it's injured. Let 'em think it's an easy meal. Perfection! We'll make a fisherman of you yet.'

He ruffled my hair. 'Everything was settled for years before the accident. The trolls never bothered anyone, and nobody bothered them back. Out of sight, out of mind.' Dar grabbed the rod and flicked it hard to the side. 'But when I broke my leg, the clan were cut off from their food supply. I couldn't just zip about getting dead chickens and scrumping apples. My body wouldn't let me. Trolls are nomadic, you see, and there's not enough food in the forest that can be foraged for the winter. So they had to break cover and find their own resources.'

He took the rod, recast perfectly across the bank, and handed it back.

'Same again and keep away from the lilies. I know you think I'm just a doddery old fool, and maybe I'm getting that way, but you could say I'm something of a warrior, like you with your arcade box.'

I reeled in fast, then slow … then fast again.

'I'll share a secret with you, seeing as I owe you my life. And that makes you a man in my book, by the way. The crash was no accident. Breaking my leg wasn't the cleverest trick, but the accident … that was an act of war! My land was invaded. And under ancient Kriger law a *feltet-tryyg*, a territory held for the safe harbouring of trollfolk, is sacred territory. It's not state land or crown land or sovereign soil. It's nothing. For all intents and purposes, it doesn't exist.'

The short rod bent double.

'WE'RE IN!' Dar yelled, and adjusted the rear drag of the reel for me.

'Gotta … keep … things … tight. WOOHOOO!'

Dar placed his hands over mine and we wrestled the fish together. The reel made an awesome metallic ripping sound as the pike fought more line from the spool.

'Come on, you beauty! Don't give him an inch, Brandon.'

Dar took the rod from me and began hopping about on the riverbank like William after too many sweets. Except Dar looked far less graceful as he struggled to stay upright, his crutch sinking into the sandy ground – still not a hundred-per-cent steady on his new robot legs, juggling crutch and fishing rod together.

'What do you mean, an act of war?' I said.

Dar mopped his brow, dancing left and right … not giving the fish an inch as the rod bent double and the line hummed like it was singing along.

'War. A battle … like this one here. Except we're the fish and Lackshaft's limpseys are the anglers.'

Dar battled closer to victory as a huge fish tail crashed against the surface, forcing a tide of ripples across the otherwise calm water.

'Except they're fishing with nets and dynamite, because they've got no punkins.'

'What are punkins anyway?' I asked, now comfortable enough to pick Dar up on his weird words.

'Punkins. Old English. It means courage or dexterity. Or balls-out, bat-shit brave … you'd probably say!'

I laughed, hearing my slang rubbing off on my ancient grandfather.

'And he, my dear boy, is positively bereft of his punkins.'

'He's a snowflake!' I added, keen to broaden Dar's vocabulary.

The rod creaked as Dar fought against the huge fish. 'Snowflake?'

'Same thing. Just another kind of melt.' I kind of wanted to turn Dar's cap back to front, but that would probably have been a step too far.

'They're cowards, one and all. They took the king's shilling.' Dar wound hard while the fish fought against the grinding drag of the reel. 'But righteousness always trumps the coin. You've got to reel 'em in. Let 'em think they're winning the fight. And then, after an epic battle, you defeat them.'

Dar yanked on the rod.

'Grab the net, boy!'

I scooped the net under a massive pike and the battle was won! Dar puffed hard and shook his fists to the heavens, winding down from the adrenaline.

'We did it, Yormagorp!'

Dar high-fived me … and it hurt!

It was an awesome creature, and it certainly had punkins, bucket-loads of them. It was almost as tall as William, with a fat white belly. Built like a torpedo, with rows of razor-sharp teeth set inside a long, tapered head. It was green and brown and spotty – an amazing camouflage – with big orange fins and a huge tail.

Dar took a sneaky look around, then knocked the pike dead with one punch. He flopped it into a sack, whistling as he gave me his little trademark eyebrow flick.

'That's supper!'

Dar was clearly filled with pride. I wasn't entirely sure if we were allowed to take the pike home. Given how he'd acted, we probably weren't.

Back at the farm, we were met by Pugwash. He was painting the old barn with creosote – another rotten-smelling product of the countryside.

'Mornin', leeky.' His one solitary top tooth seemed to dance as he spoke. 'Got in a right hugger mugger darn in the bibble last night then?' He chuckled and spat on his hands.

Dar poked him playfully in the chest. 'Are we ship-shape, old boy?'

'Lek it never 'appended, boi. Lek it never 'appened. And you,' – he ruffled my hair with a creosote-soaked hand – 'reet little fart-catcher, saving yer ole dar from a pine overcoat. Got some punkins there, boi.'

I smiled at him politely, hoping he wouldn't touch me again, although insanely proud to know I now had my fair share of punkins. He handed Dar a stack of notes and we left him to it.

As we walked away Dar chuckled, counting the money. 'Must have filled the quad-bike's petrol tank with rubble before weighing it in at the scrapyard.' Dar pulled a banknote from the stack and stuffed the rest in his waistcoat pocket. 'He's a wise one, old Pugwash. Lackshaft will be back, of that we can be certain, so we don't want any loose ends. No quad-bike, no questions!'

'Yeah, but what did he say to me? Were they actual words?'

Pugwash could literally have been chatting in Klingon.

Dar slipped me a twenty-pound note, pressing his finger to his lips.

'He said you did well,' Dar replied, ruffling my hair.

And I had.

Without asking for, or even wanting it, adventure had crept up and bitten me on the butt. I tucked the note into my trouser pocket and felt suddenly very grown-up, like I'd slithered out of my boy skin and a man had emerged – brave and strong.

CHAPTER TWELVE

An Incredible Discovery

It was early afternoon and the sun-washed birch trees shimmered like gold. The upper branches of the huge old oak rustled. Dar tightened his grip on my arm and I stared up at him. His elderly eyes sparkled like diamonds.

He pressed his finger to his lips and guided my attention back to the tree. The large wicker basket, loaded with a rank buffet of rotten apples and feathery dead chickens, remained untouched.

We didn't move a muscle. I felt brave because Dar was by my side. Plus, now I knew the family secret, nothing would ever faze me again. Besides, how could I possibly be fearful of the one thing that had saved us both last night?

It was mad, a twelve-year-old trying to make sense of it all. One of those moments where you knew it was happening but wouldn't have been surprised if you'd woken up to find out it had all been just a crazy dream. Like when I got the

Robosapien for my eleventh birthday and then, the same night, I sat at the top of the stairs and watched Dad leave. That moment on the rollercoaster when there's no way back and your butt's about to end up in the back of your throat. Or like the time I completed *Super Mario World* and I cried. It was sweet, but it was so, so sour. Look, I'm just a kid! No, it's basically like the time me and my Dar almost died and got saved by a troll … and then sat waiting at the base of an old oak tree to give him a basket of chickens as a thank-you gift.

My head was spinning so I gripped Dar's hand tight.

The upper branches rustled again. I held my breath. And then a loud snort rang out through the treetops. A bellowing snort that seemed to suck the leaves and branches into it.

And then a giant upside-down eye.

Set into the corner of a giant upside-down face.

Poking through the branches.

The kind of eye on the kind of face that had rolled in wet mud so all the sticks and mulchy leaves and beetles and worms stuck to it. It reminded me of that time William dropped his ice cream in Elveden Forest and decided to carry on eating it – woodlice and all. Euggh!

That kind of face.

We watched in pin-drop silence as the vast head slowly lowered from the branches. It just hung there, staring at us. Staring right at me.

It didn't blink. It didn't frown or twitch.

It was just there.

It hadn't been before and then it was.

Dar released his grip a little and caught my eye. He did the eyebrow thing that I do. Not the one when I'm angry with people's stupidity, but the great one – the OMG WTF-word one that gets you put in isolation at school. This was real.

But right now, I didn't have time to get my head round that.

Because we were being stared at.

By a troll.

'It's Forfaltrot,' Dar whispered.

The troll blinked and moved his head slightly towards us. Even though we were only looking at about a quarter of his head – upside down – it gave me a sense of how much of him was hidden. And while I'm not the most mathsy of kids, it was clear there a whole lot of troll in that big old tree. I suddenly didn't feel so brave, and gripped Dar's wrist a little tighter.

Forfaltrot grunted, looked down at the basket of food, and then back to us. And then, as quickly as he'd appeared, he was gone.

We sat there for a moment in silence. My head was spinning and I still had a million questions for Dar.

'What now?' I whispered when my lip had stopped quivering.

'Patience,' he said.

He reached into his coat pocket and pulled out a jar. The label said *Honey* and I had no reason to doubt the contents. Carefully, like he was defusing a bomb, Dar eased open the lid. He lay it on the ground, took my hand, and dipped my fingers into the pot. Then he nodded his head towards the tree.

I stared at him, intelligent enough to know what he wanted, and sensible enough to act dumb. He gently pushed my back, but I held fast.

'Not going to happen,' I whispered.

The tree rustled.

I froze.

Quick as a flash, Dar grabbed my honey hand and started waving it towards the tree.

What was this? Was he about to feed me to the troll, as payback for throwing the brick at the rat, making him crash the quad-bike, and nearly killing us in the process?

Terrified, I tried to pull my hand away, but Dar held firm.

I looked up at him, and saw the kindness in his eyes, and it reassured me. He rose, motioning for me to stay put, and sneaked across to the tree. I quickly licked every last drop of honey from my fingers. This wasn't about hunger. This was pure self-preservation.

Dar huddled by the base of the tree and smeared honey over the basket. He was childlike now, all excitable and breathless; my old grandfather sneaking around in the dirt like a man a quarter of his age. He stole back through the bracken and crouched beside me.

'Now, you watch carefully, my boy.'

His hand found mine and I felt safe again. It seemed like we waited ages, but it was probably only about a minute until the branches rustled.

I heard a huge sniff and then the huge troll flopped from the tree with a ground-trembling thud. He landed in a squat, his two huge gnarly knees touching. He was enormous – easily twice as tall as Dar and maybe even bigger than the lime-green combine harvester. No wonder he'd popped us on top of the straw stack with such ease.

I'd never seen a troll before … well, except the glimpse when I was barely conscious. I'd only heard about them through Dar's bedtime stories to William or seen the bad ones in the movies.

Of course I hadn't. Trolls didn't exist. Yet, here one was, no more than ten metres away from us. A real-life troll … and he was freaking awesome. A gargantuan blend of Wookie and tree. The troll before my eyes could most certainly have done with a damned good pressure wash; it was hard to tell where the forest stopped and the troll began.

Forfaltrot leaned forward and sniffed the basket. It rattled vigorously and a few chicken feathers disappeared up the troll's nose. I looked at Dar. He gently placed his hand under my jaw to close my mouth, then wiped away a bit of dribble with his dirty jumper cuff.

I was mesmerised. Here I was, standing in the middle of a forest with my boring old grandfather, staring at a real-life troll. And, man, his buttocks were massive. Fat Tina, Jamie's mum, was some blubbery mass of a woman but her buttocks look like peanuts compared with Forfaltrot's.

The troll reached forward and plucked a chicken from the bushel, pinching it between his fingers like I would a garden pea. Each finger was the size of a Subway roll and crowned with a huge claw of a fingernail. And then the chicken was gone. He hadn't chewed, hadn't gulped, hadn't done anything really, just opened up his huge mouth and the chicken was no more.

Then another, and another, and another.

Dar shuffled a little closer, pulling me with him.

Forfaltrot stopped eating and stared at us.

'No, Dar,' I whispered.

'Trust me,' he said, and held the pot of honey towards the giant troll. We inched closer and closer. 'He'll stay this time. Nice and slow. And don't stare into his eyes for too long.'

The troll looked up and supported himself on his fists, just like the big Silverback gorilla I'd seen in Colchester Zoo at Shane's birthday party the previous month. He stretched his neck forward and sniffed the air around us. We were now about twenty feet away.

I'd never seen anything like him. *He* was obviously a mammal, sort of like an ancient human, a troglodyte, but it was as if he'd been genetically fused with nature. There were tree roots and ivy growing down his arms, and his chin was a mixture of matted hair and grass.

Dar got to his feet and dragged me with him. It must have been like dragging like a dog who didn't want to walk. By the time we got to the base of the oak my adrenaline had kicked in.

My legs were jellified. I stood, rooted to the spot, while Forfaltrot nuzzled his face into Dar's body, almost toppling him over. Then he picked Dar up in his huge hand and turned him slowly around in front of his eyes, like he was giving him my grandfather a thorough inspection.

The flesh on the troll's hand was torn and red raw. Dar noticed it too and reached his own hand out to touch the wound. Forfaltrot winced and shared a second of eye contact with Dar; his piercing eyes were drenched with sadness and I instantly felt a wave of emotion for him. Or from him – it was like he'd plugged a USB into my mind from his own. He placed Dar carefully back on the ground and traced his finger along the length of my grandfather's leg.

'I'm fine. Honestly, it's fine.'

I'm certain Forfaltrot understood Dar's words because he pressed his face into Dar's and licked him. The troll's tongue was the size of a shovel.

Then he spoke … I think. It certainly wasn't a roar … more a soft and caring murmur – words I had no chance of understanding. The gruff, bassy mumbles of a language from another world.

'I wanted to thank you for saving us.' Dar reached out and held the pot of honey towards Forfaltrot. 'I wanted you to know we are grateful.'

The troll's ears swivelled towards the sound of Dar's voice.

'Very grateful indeed.'

Forfaltrot dropped to the forest floor. The sheer scale of this amazing creature totally blew my mind. His hairy buttocks could easily have filled William's new paddling pool and his head was the size of Auntie Jenny's car. He took the honeypot from Dar's hand and looked right at me. I avoided eye contact and he leaned forward, taking a mighty sniff of my head. I felt my hair disappearing up his nostrils.

But I wasn't scared. Not anymore.

And then Forfaltrot rose to his feet, grabbed the bushel of stinking food, placed the honeypot in the bushel and disappeared into the branches of the tree.

A few leaves fluttered to the ground, then all was still.

Wide-eyed, I stared at Dar, my body bristling with adrenaline. Forfaltrot. To see, smell, touch such a magnificent creature … it was awesome. And although I'd decided to allow myself to believe that trolls are real, it was nice to have it confirmed indisputably.

I stared up at my grandfather.

'Do you think he understands us?'

Dar nodded. 'Absolutely. But in ways I could never begin to explain.'

Now I needed to know more. Everything.

I needed to help my grandparents stay safe.

I needed to feel what it meant to be a Kriger in its truest sense.

I needed to find my punkins … and step up!

CHAPTER THIRTEEN

The Doctor's Discretion

Later that afternoon, I spent time in my room; chillaxing. I tried reading, gaming, chatting to Shane online, but nothing stopped my head spinning at a hundred miles an hour.

So, if trolls existed, what else might be real? All the things I'd thought were fantasy … what of them? Werewolves, zombies, the tooth fairy, the Easter bunny. God, the devil, heaven, hell. Even *the Stickybin*, that Mum said the security guards in the shopping centre would chuck us in if we didn't *shut the hell up*.

I took a monster hit of Rescue Remedy and lay down very, very still. Normally it washed over me like a soothing cuddle from someone I trusted with my life, but not today. I was consumed by my thoughts. And it was all too much.

My anxiety counsellor had once told me that it didn't pay to overthink things, but I'd have liked to have seen the inner workings of her brain if she'd just witnessed what I had. I seriously needed to rethink my entire worldview.

Dar knocked on my door and entered with Dr Saunders. It was an extremely welcome distraction. My first thought was to cling onto him and beg for a higher dose of anxiety pills, but I thought better of it.

The doctor's nose was awesome – one of those features you knew you shouldn't look at too much as it wasn't good manners. But, sheesh, what a snout. Huge and bumpy, with a network of blue veins all over it: the kind of nose Dar said showed an 'overt fondness of alcohol. Like a roadmap to excess'. But he seemed nice enough and quickly put me at ease, checking me over to ensure there was no lasting damage from the accident.

I was also extremely reassured to hear that Dar was fine. His ankle was sprained, and the cuts were superficial. My own bruising would disappear within a few days, so things were far less tragic than I'd feared. The doctor stared at me, and offered a thin-lipped smile, while I fought to ignore his giant schnozz.

'You've certainly been making a name for yourself, young man.' The doctor ruffled my hair. 'Your grandfather and I go a long way back, so we're all friends here.' He pumped the blood-pressure cuff around Dar's arm, checking the gauge as it inflated. 'I imagine a boy of your age might be carrying an element of bewilderment. Am I correct?' I looked at Dar for clarity. 'Villages are curious places. Not always as they seem.' He deflated the cuff and placed it back in his leather case. 'And for a boy of the town … does that sit kindly?'

I shrugged.

'The child's good, Doctor.' Dar patted my knee. 'He's a clever boy. He'll make sense of it. In his own time.'

The doctor handed Dar a small bottle of pills.

'Three a day with food and you'll be right as rain.'

The doctor's bones clicked as he rose, and Dar signalled me to leave with them, squinting a warning as I eyeballed the doctor's nose.

We took the Land Rover across Flossy's Field. Dar was clearly still in discomfort but I'd learned that farmers are as hard as rock. And Dar was one of the toughest – despite his years. I sat in the back, holding on for all my worth as the rutted field made my teeth clatter.

'This takes me back.' The doctor smiled at Dar. 'Crikey. Must have been nineteen sixty … seven.'

Dar whistled his disbelief.

'Seems like yesterday. Just past lambing season,' Dar said.

I watched Pitchbury Wood growing closer, wondering what other lifelong beliefs might be flipped upside today.

'*Sergeant Pepper* was released, remember?' The doctor began humming and Dar whistled along. They looked so ancient – two elderly men chattering together like me and my mates did. I'd always thought old people were dumb. Pointless even. How wrong I'd been.

Dar was epic! A warrior for the troll people. I wondered what kind of Kriger Dar was, back in the day, in his youth … though I still wasn't entirely sure what a Kriger was. Maybe Dar was like The Rock, or Vin Diesel, some kind of badass Kriger warrior kickin' butts and takin' names. I thought back to the awesome battleaxe in the toolshed, Snaghorn, wondering whether Dar had used it to cleave off the heads of his enemies. I absolutely needed that battleaxe!

Leaving the Land Rover at the edge of the forest, we walked the short distance to the base of the old oak. There was no sign of trolls, chickens, feathers – just forest. We sat at the foot of the tree and waited. And waited. And waited! Dar pulled a small jar from his pocket.

'God's nectar!' He tossed it to the doctor and seemed proud as his friend unscrewed the lid and dipped his finger in the pot.

'She's still bottling the finest honey in East Anglia then?' The doctor tasted the honey and pretended to pass out with happiness. 'The druids believed that bees were divine messengers from the gods. Did you know that, child?'

The doctor waved the pot in my direction until I dipped my own finger in and tasted. An explosion of flavour tore through my senses, kissing my taste buds like cool rain on the hottest day. Sweetness, fields, flowers, sunshine. I nodded my head eagerly, scooping globs of honey from the pot and stuffing them into my mouth.

The doctor laughed. 'Steady, boy. Can't have you slipping into a honey frenzy. Not here. Not now.'

Dar took the pot from the doctor's hand and screwed on the cap.

'Hilde's got a bottle of braggot back at the farmhouse for you, Ned.' Dar gave the doctor one of his special eyebrow lifts, the way he did. My way. It told me they were great friends.

'And I shall drink to your good health.'

Dar launched the honeypot towards a mound of earth a few metres across the forest.

'Remember the day we lost the hives?' Dar said.

'Aye,' the doctor replied. 'Three wayward trolls brought to heel by an army of vengeful bees.' They laughed together for a moment. 'None so pitiful as a drunken troll.'

Dar leaned close into me. 'As mighty and fearsome as a troll might be, my little habbadehoy, let him loose on a quart of honey and he's a wastrel.' I stared at Dar, confused. 'Can't handle their honey you see, Brandon. Or too many rotten apples. And they do make for despicable drunks!'

'They say that in times gone by' – the doctor leaned into me conspiratorially – 'the knights who held the finest bees commanded the trolls, and the knights who controlled the trolls commanded the land.'

I mentally pinched myself. Here was I, a twelve-year-old lad, bearing witness to quite possibly the most extraordinary truths in the world. I suddenly felt very grown-up … and a little anxious. My hand found Dar's.

'A lesson in life, my boy. A lesson in moderation. A pipette to attract and a spoon to adhere.' The doctor spluttered as he spoke, and I couldn't help but wonder whether he'd have had a nicer nose if he'd taken his own advice.

He was such was an excitable little man. He bobbed up and down as he spoke and kept tapping the bridge of his glasses to keep them in place … another thing a normal nose was good for.

'Trolls are fiercely loyal, my boy! But it doesn't pay to overplay the honey bargaining. There's none worse than a clan of trolls in the midst of a honey frenzy. You just ask your old Dar. He still bears the scars from the day his hives fell.'

'So you do know about the trolls then?' I knew he did – it was obvious – but my reeling mind still craved confirmation. Just to be absolutely sure.

'Course I do, my dear child. He's somewhat of a hero, your old Dar. Many a wound I've stitched over the decades. Some deeper than others, but that's your grandfather … and Hilde!' The doctor pointed to Dar. 'That, my boy, is what a real superhero looks like.'

'Pah!' Dar seemed embarrassed by the praise. 'We do what we do, right?'

'We do what we do.' The doctor placed his arm round Dar's shoulder. 'And then I fix him … when things get a bit tasty.' He paused for a moment and then chuckled. '*We do what we do,*' he whispered. 'Only a hero would say that.'

It seemed Dar had a fan club. And deservedly so.

Then something spectacular happened. The mound of earth by the honeypot rose, just like the lid of Nana Biddle's stove, exposing a hole in the ground. Dar climbed to his feet, brushed himself down and straightened his bones.

'That's us. It's time to meet a troll, my little habbadehoy!'

CHAPTER FOURTEEN

Trolldom

The tunnel was wide enough for the three of us to walk side by side. Just tall enough for Dar's outstretched fingers to rake across the veiny, rooted ceiling. And it was waaay too dark.

Dar's head torch illuminated our way, emitting a comforting circle of white light that stopped me from stumbling too much over the roots and stumps. I pulled out my mobile phone, switched on the flashlight and moved it to the lowest setting – mindful not to waste battery power – lest my super masterplan fell flat at the first phase.

I'd been planning since breakfast, even more so since Dar confirmed that Forfaltrot could understand us. I'm a tech-boy; tech is my life. And mobile phones? They are epic. They're not just for calling, Instagramming and Snapchatting. They're cameras, audio and video recorders, translators … everything. And that was the foundation of my masterplan.

Like all good almost-thirteen-year-olds, I needed to know everything, and my mobile phone held the key to supreme knowledge.

In the distance, a faint light shone. I felt sure we were heading downwards, a slow descent into something unknown.

Dar gripped my hand tightly. And I held tight right back.

'Does anyone else know about the trolls, Dar?'

He led me though the darkened tunnel.

'Just us,' he said.

'And what about Nana Biddle and Mum?' I knew I was privileged to hold this new information but, like every young lad, I needed specifics – just so I could be absolutely certain how special I was.

My eyes had now adjusted to the darkness but that did little to ease my concern. I was totally out of my comfort zone. A dank, dark, stinking place … and I didn't like it one bit! The walls felt like they were closing in on me and I felt very, very small.

'Your mother isn't as resilient as you might think, my little habbadehoy. She can't know too much. Do you understand?'

'No, I don't.' I wasn't being difficult. I really didn't.

We entered a large open space. I couldn't see any lights or fires and yet it was lit. Not flicked-light-switch bright, not enough to read or tie a fishing lure by … just a warm, gentle light.

'Your mother is fragile, Brandon,' the doctor said. 'It would be detrimental to her health, is what your Dar's trying to say. And we don't be wanting that, do we now?'

I shook my head.

Small openings led off the perimeter of the space. There were beds made of straw and forest leaves, piles of stuff, and an overwhelming stench of rotten egg. It felt like we were in the belly of the troll's … I want to say home, but it wasn't very homely at all. It wasn't much of anything really and I suddenly felt very sad for them.

'And what about Nana Biddle?'

Dar didn't answer my question, just snapped his torch onto my head. I switched off my phone light to save the battery.

'Dar, does Nana Biddle know about the trolls?' I said, punctuating my question with urgency as I looked around.

There were further signs of life … carvings on the walls, crude etchings like the ones we'd studied in Ancient History last autumn for our Mesolithic project. There was a huge fireplace. The hearth had been moulded from clay and decorated with fragments of old tiles and flint. It was full of charred logs. I placed my hand over them; they were still warm. The fireplace stood proudly in the middle of the room. And, yes, it most certainly was a room.

The doctor crouched and riffled through his medicine bag.

It wasn't a room in the sense of the ones we all know and live in, day to day. This was a troll's room, the heart of a troll home. And you know what? I was good with that. Because I was, after all, possibly one of only three people in England privileged enough to hold this extraordinary knowledge.

I aimed my head torch at Dar, causing him to shield his eyes.

'Dar? I asked if Nana Biddle knows. Does she?'

He puffed out a hard breath, still ignoring me, and tilted my head towards the ceiling. The light bounced off, and a million stars seemed to twinkle, just like William's turtle light.

'Woah. What are they? Are they jewels?' I asked. 'Buttons, Dar! They're shiny buttons, like the ones in Nana Biddle's button box … and glued to the trees in the chicken paddock.'

They'd been stuck in everywhere, creating the most wonderful shimmering display of light all over the ceiling.

'Now, stop asking so many stupid questions!' Dar grabbed my collar and ushered me down another tunnel off the main room.

What I witnessed next blew my mind!

This second chamber was similar to the first but divided into separate rooms, like our camping tent – a middle bit with a high ceiling and three smaller cubbyholes leading off.

I aimed the head torch up and found more buttons twinkling on the ceiling. There must have been thousands! I craned my neck back as far as I could. The view was dazzling. It must have taken years. Was there a connection with Nana Biddle's button-gluing obsession and the trolldom ceiling buttons? I was sure there was but was too engrossed to offer it much thought. I'd save it for later when I was less occupied and in a less eggy environment!

And then all thoughts of buttons, glue and Nana Biddle vanished …

Because huddled in one of the alcoves were two trolls. Much smaller, more childlike. Their skin was soft and pale and glistening, not gnarled and rooty like Forfaltrot's. The little trolls cowered as my torchlight landed on them. The beam bounced off their irises like the little rubber cats-eyes in the middle of a motorway. They shielded their faces, squealing like scared little pigs, as Dar grabbed the torch from my head.

'You'll blind them!' His voice was laced with anger. 'Hold it down, like this!' Dar shone the light on the floor and the two young trolls timidly returned to dipping their thumbs in honey and sucking on them noisily.

The doctor approached and handed them a few lumps of sugar. 'They need to stay underground, child, the young-uns. Light blinds them, so we try and expediate their retinal efficiency with a blend of zeaxanthin, vitamins C and E and carotene drops.' Doctor Saunders leaned into me and whispered, 'Hidden in a harmless little sugar lump. They'll develop a tolerance to moonlight first.'

I looked up at him. 'Like gremlins!'

'Whatever they are. But I'll take you by your word.'

The doctor and Dar really did need to get some telly time under their belts. I knelt just outside the small trolls' alcove and waited for my eyes to adjust, considering whether to ask the doctor for a couple of sugar lumps for myself.

'We'll be just behind you, my little habbadehoy. The doctor's just got to iodine Forfaltrot's wounds.'

I turned around, amazed to discover that what I'd initially assumed to be a huge mound of earth and rock was actually the giant troll who'd saved our lives. The troll mountain came to life before my eyes. I glanced back at the young trolls; they were watching me with unflinching interest. I rose, very carefully, and approached the giant as Dar held my shoulder, controlling the speed of my approach.

I could now sense Forfaltrot's breathing. Slow. Laboured. A giant wheezy bellow that sounded a bit like Darth Vader through an amplifier. A huge eye opened. And then I was face to face with a troll who, lying down, was easily bigger than Uncle Martin's fishing boat. (Uncle Martin, who I'd found out wasn't an uncle at all. Mum had introduced me to several new uncles over the past year or so, but Uncle Martin was standout … because he had his own boat and greeted everyone with a cheery 'Ahoy!' So much friendlier than what's-his-face.)

'I … I wanted to thank you.' I cleared my throat, allowing my big voice to break through, and leant forward, gently outstretching a clammy hand. 'I wanted to thank you for saving us.'

Forfaltrot lifted his head and took a big sniff. I felt the skin of my cheek pull slightly away from my face and towards his giant nostril. Then he licked my face! His tongue was a thousand time rougher than Lil's. I thought it might pull my cheek off, but, luckily, everything stayed where it was.

Then all I could smell was egg.

'I thought trolls weren't real … and didn't really want them to be. But now I know …' I gently stroked his face with the back of my hand, fearless because – and I don't know why, or how – I could sense his kindness from deep within my heart. 'I just wanted to thank you.' I felt a tear roll down my cheek. 'I know now … that trolls exist. And I'm so very glad for it.'

Then he spoke! It was low, rumbly, incoherent. Foreign and ancient. But they *were* words, and he spoke them. And I recorded every sound and every ancient rumble on my mobile phone.

The wheels of my super-tech masterplan were in motion.

CHAPTER FIFTEEN

Enemy at the Gates

I walked with my shortest stride. This was to be a short journey filled with as many questions as a boy could ask in the very shortest of time. Questions that must be answered!

'Troll babies, Dar. But how can a troll baby be fifty years old? A baby is six, ten months … a year maybe. Not fifty.' I glanced up, my eyes surely twinkling bright with curiosity.

Dar stopped in his tracks and stared down at me. 'So how old do you think Forfaltrot is?'

'Your age?'

Dar and the doctor laughed. 'A troll father is as old as the greatest oak, my little habbedehoy. He might be five hundred harvests. A thousand even! There really is no way of telling.'

I dragged my heels, knowing that the moment we neared the old farmhouse the inquisition would end.

'And you've always known about this?' I'm sure by now that my eyes must have been popping out on stalks. The only probable difference between me and some crusty old crab now was that I wasn't scuttling sideways, clicking my pincers.

'My grandfather, your great, great grandfather, made a pact with the troll clan.' Dar pulled me close and knelt before me. 'There is nobody alive today who knows this, Brandon, but myself, Nana Biddle and the good doctor here.' He placed his arms on my shoulders.

So Nana Biddle was in on this amazing secret too. I was instantly disappointed, because my exclusivity percentage had suddenly dropped from thirty-three to twenty-five.

'You, my dear child, are a Ballard. And I trust you with my life. But most importantly I trust your integrity. I trust that you'll never, ever breathe a word of this to anyone. Especially your parents! Do I have your word?'

I nodded emphatically.

'Good! Good boy.'

The doctor helped Dar hobble over the broken fence that led from the forest and back into Flossy's Field, and then slowly towards the Land Rover. Questions brewed in my mind.

'Ned delivered the troll twins and has helped guard the Ballard family secret ever since. Like an honorary Kriger!'

The doctor waved away the praise while I stopped in my tracks.

'Does he have a Kriger axe too? Like Snaghorn.'

Dar scoffed and continued walking. I raced to catch up. 'Surely a man with trolls could have everything, Dar. Can you control them, like an army commander?'

He pondered my question, then span around theatrically, waving his arms towards the trees.

'Tell me, Brandon, what more could a man want?'

'A better tractor perhaps.' My sarcasm fell on deaf ears.

'I pledged to protect the clan from persecution and certain death. What better prize than peace of mind, my little habbadehoy?'

He ushered me into the back of the Land Rover, leaving me to muse over the greater rewards of having my own troll bodyguard. I gripped the dirty rope strap that hung from the ceiling and clenched my teeth. *Maybe some better suspension wouldn't go amiss.*

I felt inside my inner coat pocket, just to be sure the mobile phone was still there. I was itching to get back to my room.

The Land Rover came to an abrupt halt. Dar climbed out and looked up, shielding his eyes. Then I heard the whirring. My eyes followed the noise and I saw a helicopter high in the sky, circling like a kestrel on the hunt.

'Stay inside, child.' The doctor smiled at me and then joined Dar outside.

I pressed my face against the window, feeling the cool glass on my cheeks as the helicopter grew larger and descended gracefully. The long grass flattened, bowing its admiration to the huge rotors above.

I'd never seen a helicopter this close before. It was amazing! But Dar and the doctor didn't seem to share my fascination.

The blades slowed, came to a halt, and then all was quiet. The door opened and Councillor Lackshaft squeezed himself through the door – an opening clearly not designed for a man of his bulk. Two more immaculately dressed men followed. It was weird to see men on a farm wearing suits instead of the usual grungy oil-slicked overalls and ripped straw-covered jumpers. These men weren't dressed for the outdoors; they were dressed for business. And not good business, if the expressions on the faces of my grandfather and Doctor Saunders were anything to go by.

Dar straightened himself tall and approached the men, arm outstretched for a cheery handshake.

I loved the way he knew how to be … even when it wasn't the way he wanted to be. I'm sure he wanted nothing more than to grab the fat councillor by his ears and knee him in the balls. Maybe Dar's handshake had a little more squeeze than one he might give to someone he didn't wish to knee in the balls. But there he stood, with a broad smile, pumping the councillor's hand like they were the very best of friends. It was *subterfuge*. Dar had taught me this after the councillor's last visit. Deceit used in order to achieve one's goals. I liked the word but loved its meaning more. I'd used this technique several times myself when recruiting *Clash of Clans* allies, only to block them when I'd achieved my own goals. I just hadn't put a name to it.

Dar was actually pretty street for a man of the land.

I looked at the two men behind the councillor. Maybe they were his bodyguards, like the ones that had been all over Prince Harry and Megan's royal wedding. Secret-service people. They wore badges, like the ones we wore when we went to Essex university for Science Week. One held a clipboard and the other had a moustache the size of a squirrel. I wondered what I might look like with a squirrel moustache, and decided that if I did choose to sport a hairy face when I was older, I'd probably have one of the upside-down horseshoe ones like badasses have.

I'd make a great badass – especially riding about on the back of a troll. *Aiden Hunt* wouldn't stand a chance. I'd ride down the sports-hall corridor, calling him out, waving Snaghorn above my head, roaring my Kriger battle-cry through a badass moustache.

All badass and troll.

And I'd crush that bullying moron to chalk dust. Mister Reynolds would shout out, 'Come down here this second, boy!' And I'd just laugh, turn my troll around and ride out of there. Probably to an epic soundtrack … like Skrillex or Chase & Status. A heavy bass track for a badass trollrider!

The Land Rover window had steamed up. The conversation had become quite animated and Lackshaft was waving the clipboard in Dar's face. I wiped the window with my sleeve and pulled out my mobile phone. I swiped the screen, tapped the camera and zoomed right in. Mobile phones also made great binoculars!

Dar was red-faced and not quite as friendly as when he'd offered the first handshake. The doctor stood a step or two behind him. Clearly, he hadn't been built for confrontation, though with that nose I'm certain he could comfortably take a punch or two.

Squirrel Moustache poked his finger towards Dar's face; nastily. Dar grabbed it and the man dropped to his knees. Things were certainly getting heated. The next thing I knew, my legs had run me to his side.

'If you think you can just turn up on my farm in your metal bird with more wild accusations, you've got another think coming.' Dar's head was shaking, his veins glowing red. Full-on Jurassic mode.

'Unhand my colleague, Mr Ballard.' The councillor wrestled with Dar's hand, but Dar held fast. Ten hands couldn't release Dar's iron-like grip. Maybe it was one of his robot hands!

'If you've got hot shadows or thermals or whatever on your cameras then that's your problem, Basil. It's no fault of mine.' Dar released the man's finger and stepped nose-to-nose with the fat councillor. 'Throw your notions of creatures or God knows whatever else is in that addled mind of yours to another wind. Because they WILL NOT stick here.'

Lackshaft took a nervous step back and tentatively held the clipboard up to my grandfather again.

'So explain to me … explain to me, *Farmer Ballard*, how here,' – he flicked to another page – 'here' – and another – 'and here, thermal imaging clearly shows an object of some dimension moving at a considerable pace, over a distance of some eight hundred metres in the hours of darkness. Where it has no time or place to be.'

Dar didn't respond. Neither did the doctor.

'And we can clearly see your tractor, Land Rover and all other farm vehicles safely tucked away for the night. So you tell me, dear Mister Ballard, in the absence of vehicles, hot air balloons,' – he leaned into Dar's ear – 'triceratops or diplodocus, what might be prowling your fields in the dead of night?'

Dar's breathing increased. I saw the flex in his jaw followed by a slow clench of his fist. I imagined that any moment the fat councillor might be smashed in the face by my grandfather.

'Bees, sir.'

I stepped forward, a small but bold step, and cleared my throat. 'They were bees.'

There was silence as every eye turned in my direction.

'The swarm was on the move. From one hive field to the next.'

The silence continued.

'It's plausible.' One of the suited men took the clipboard from the councillor and examined the images.

Dar side-glanced me, the corners of his mouth creeping up a fraction.

'It would explain why I saw so many scout bees by the stacks this past week,' Dar chipped in, puckering his lips and fixing his gaze on Lackshaft, as though deep in thought.

The councillor's face dropped, and the colour drained from his cheeks as he turned to his allies.

'And how many bees might you have, Mister Ballard?' His words came out hard, angry, laced with bitterness – like he was slurping sick through a straw.

'Twenty … thirty thousand to a hive.' Dar counted on his fingers. 'Twelve hives across two fields.' His fingers continued their walk, but I knew maths wasn't his best subject. 'Many, many bees, Councillor. Many bees indeed.'

Squirrel Moustache tapped away on a calculator. 'That's three hundred thousand bees, sir.'

The other official whistled through his teeth. 'That's some mass, Councillor. Some heat. Three hundred thousand bees, you say?' He rubbed his chin in contemplation.

'Sounds about right.' Dar nodded slowly, confident and poised.

The doctor stepped forward and rested his hand on Dar's shoulder. 'So perhaps this concludes your investigation, Councillor Lackshaft. As unexpected as it was. I'm sure we've all got better things to be doing on such a lovely evening.' He placed his hand on the councillor's back and led him, like a very good friend, towards the helicopter. 'Is Angela well? I trust she's responding to her medication.' The doctor patted Lackshaft's back as he guided him towards the door. 'You must remind me to drop by the church house with a few bottles of that elderberry linctus she enjoys so much.'

And with that the councillor and his officials were in the helicopter. Lackshaft rotated his fingers to the pilot, signalling take-off but his eyes never left my grandfather's.

We didn't wait around to watch them leave.

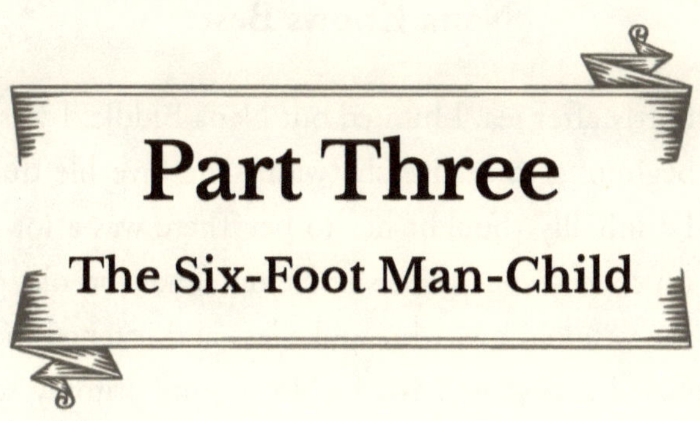

Part Three

The Six-Foot Man-Child

CHAPTER SIXTEEN

Nana Knows Best

Shortly after tea, I hunted out Nana Biddle. I was now beginning to realize she wasn't the loveable dummy I'd initially thought her to be. There was a lot more going on in her cogs than she let on. Like the old poem about the wise old owl who spoke less and listened more. I remembered it because Miss Parkinson, my primary-school teacher, had quoted it all day, every day, so the kids would stop her ears from melting.

The big dining room had been converted into Nana Biddle's bedroom a few years back after she'd slipped on the ice and broken her hip.

I knocked on the door and waited, remembering my manners. The last time I'd walked straight in I'd been met by the horrific sight of my dear grandmother sitting naked on the commode. And trust me – if a twelve-year-old boy sees his grandmother in that state of undress it hurts both eyes and all the other senses too.

Very much so.

Hearing Nana Biddle humming, I lifted the heavy iron latch and eased the open the door.

'I'm coming in, Nana.' *For the love of God, woman, please have some clothes on*, my mind screamed.

Thankfully, she was dressed. She sat at the end of the big oak dining table, working on something, her narrow shoulders hunched into the job. She looked tiny; like Yoda crossed with the Psammead from *Five Children and It*. I planted a kiss on her cheek. Her skin felt like warm Angel Delight.

She'd found my Match Attax cards and was stapling them, one by one, to an old blanket. Good old Nana Biddle. I could always count on her to find extremely creative ways to demonstrate her complete and utter madness.

I pulled out one of the fancy chairs and sat next to her. Although I was only twelve, her company always made me feel very tall, and for a boy of my age feeling tall was high on the list of priorities. Nana Biddle was no more than four-foot-six, so I suppose it really didn't count for much.

'I've had a good day today, Nana. A strange day, but good all the same. And you?'

She shrugged and stapled Paul Pogba to the blanket, next to Mark Albrighton. They hardly deserved to occupy the same midfield blanket space but I let that slide when I noticed she'd created a hem from cheese slices … threaded with one of my shoelaces.

'You know, Nana, we went up to Pitchbury Wood today.' I leaned in closer.

She chewed a stray piece of fingernail as I spoke.

'And we went under the forest too.'

Nana spat the fingernail into a handkerchief, wrapped it, and placed it in her cardigan pocket.

'Your buttons make the ceiling shine like diamonds.'

She stopped stapling.

'You can trust me, Nana. You can both trust me to keep the Ballard family secret. I need to help protect the trolls from Lackshaft.'

She placed her hand over mine and stared deep into my eyes. Her mouth puckered up like a cat's bum. But she didn't speak.

Nana Biddle never spoke.

I didn't even know if she could speak. I just assumed that some kind of illness had crossed her wires or something. I didn't really know what she understood either. All I did know was that Dar loved her very, very much and it was never spoken of.

She rose and went to the spider cupboard in the corner of the room. The spider cupboard was where the spider lived. I went in there once to find a record to play but found the spider instead. Or the spider found me. Spiders, like rats, on a farm are very well-fed monsters indeed. They grow considerably bigger than their city brothers and sisters and are built to scare. I never went in the spider cupboard again.

She crouched down by the cupboard and thumbed through a wall of records.

I waited for the spider attack. It didn't materialise. Nana Biddle pulled out a record – a blank sleeve with several words written neatly across the faded cover in black pen: *Hilde Oppegard – Beroligende Sjelen.*

Nana began humming and traced her finger across the words. Her dirty fingernail, poking from the end of her fingerless gloves, made a hideous scratching noise on the record cover.

'What is it, Nana? What does it mean?' I asked, wishing I understood gibberish. I'm certain our relationship might have been a little richer for the experience.

She closed the cupboard, scaling it's face like a climbing wall as she clambered to her feet. Meanwhile, I covertly sifted through the pile of Match Attax cards, rushing to rescue Jamie Vardy, Eden Hazard and Jonjo Shelvey before Nana Biddle condemned them to a damn good stapling.

And then the most beautiful music filled the room.

It was foreign, and ancient, and warming, and sad. It was loving and gentle … and it made me feel like crying.

My brain didn't understand a word, but my heart did.

I didn't notice where Nana Biddle went next because there were a thousand invisible strings connecting me to the sound that came from the Radiogram. I'd thought I hated old music, but this song reached the pit of me.

Then Nana was back in her seat, rocking gently in time to the beautiful score. She clutched a small bundle of blankets and hummed along. I looked at her as she stared down at the blankets, smiling to them. Her voice was perfectly in tune with the singing, mirroring the beautiful sound as if it played from her own lips.

And then it hit me.

'Nana. This is you! This is you singing, *isn't it?*'

She nodded slowly and rocked the blankets in her arms. She carefully peeled away a layer to revealed two small homemade dolls. They were crafted from sackcloth. Each had shining button eyes. Two perfect little trolls. I stared at the dolls, fascinated.

'What language is it, Nana?'

She puckered her lips and placed her finger on them. A *shush*, and the first time I'd ever got something close to a sensible interaction with her. She lay the dolls tenderly on the table and shuffled over to the old bookshelf in the corner.

I took the opportunity to stealth-search through my Match Attax cards and find Petr Cech. I lay him front and centre by the stapler. He deserved it most because of his stupid hat.

Nana returned to the table with two books. The first was a small dictionary … Norwegian to English. The second was a tattered handmade book with foreign handwriting on the front. I flicked through – the same writing filled the pages.

Nana Biddle wasn't mad!

She knew about the trolls. She knew about books, records, staplers, singing. And she was trying to tell me something. I wasn't sure what, but I was damned sure I'd find out.

I looked into the sparkly button-like eyes set deep inside her wrinkly face. I'd never really known if anything was going on in there, but the life I saw there now told me all I needed to know.

I hugged her, tucked the books and the record cover under my arm and raced to my room.

CHAPTER SEVENTEEN

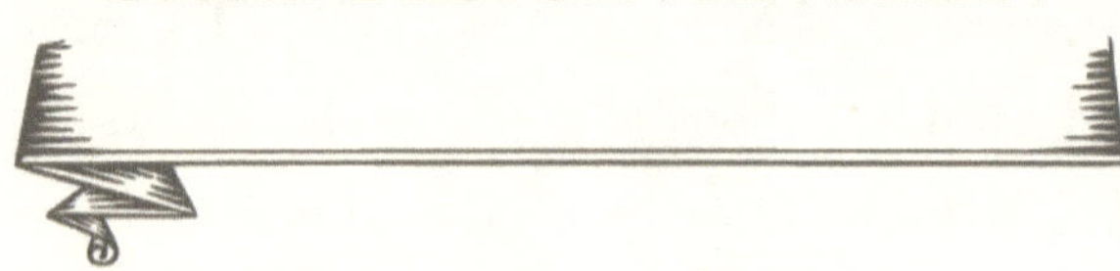

The Unlikely Scholar

My tablet was fully charged.

I pulled one of the heavy chairs up against the door and army-rolled onto the bed. My tablet powered up at supersonic speed. A click and a swipe later, I was messaging Aayush.

ME: *Wots that translate app u use?*

He wasn't quick to answer, but it gave me a chance to organize my masterplan tools.

AAYUSH: *Playing smite … so quick* ☹ *Wassup?*

ME: *That app for when your Dadima's over from Mauritius.*

AAYUSH: *iTranslate. But pa got the early beta from work and patched it, so it's got more languages.*

ME: *Can you get me it?*

AAYUSH: *Doubt it. He'd skin me. Not even released yet. He'd lose his job* ☹

ME: *I really need it. Like, really really!*

AAYUSH: *Nope. Game time brah. Only get an hour! If he found out, my PS4 would be off limits till Doomsday.*

My bed took the brunt of my frustration. A pile of dust puffed up around my fist.

ME: *I'll give you my 4-LOM pop-head if it's with me in five minutes! Pleeeease!!!*

AAYUSH: *Throw in your Fallout Pip-Boy and we have a deal.*

ME: *OK. But need asap!!!!!! Getting interesting here!*

AAYUSH: *First thing tomorrow when I can get on his laptop.*

ME: *Tonight!!!*

AAYUSH: *Too risky. He works on it most of the night. First thing. Promise.*

ME: *OK. Will have to do.*

AAYUSH: *Y so desperate?*

ME: *If I told U, I'd have to kill U! Tell you about it later. Gotta go. Thanx.*

That sucked balls! I was sitting on possibly the most awesome secret in the world, but now I just had to wait. I looked at the old book and dictionary lying on my bed and wondered what mysteries were hiding inside. But that would have to wait for a while.

I plugged my phone into the Toxic Slab with the small USB I kept in the top drawer. I booted up my tablet and it was ready to go – like a rocket. I switched the operating system from Android to Windows, opened my Video Studio software and dragged the recording file onto the desktop. I waited for the program to boot.

I was a pretty awesome editor. My YouTube channel, MrMeighem, had hundreds of subscribers and I made all my own thumbnails, intros and soundtracks. Dad even got me my own branded T-shirts to wear … like *Morgz* or *Jacksepticeye*. My best live stream had over two hundred likes!

I dragged the recording into the timeline and hit play …

Dar warning the doctor to watch his step.

Me getting told off for shining the torch.

Muffled talking.

And then: '*I just wanted to thank you. I know now … that trolls exist. And I'm so very glad for it.*' It was me, talking to Forfaltrot.

I turned up the volume and leaned in close – almost trembling with anticipation. The low, rumbling words of a troll!

I marked the speech on the audio timeline and deleted everything around it. I was left with twelve seconds.

I opened up the speed/time-lapse dropdown and sped up the recording by ten … fifteen … twenty-five … forty per cent.

Then I hit play.

Forfaltrot was speaking – actual words!

I checked my phone for messages, emails or Snapchat. There was nothing back from Aayush yet. Damn!

Never had I been more impatient for something. I saved the recording and chucked my tablet on the bed, ready for phase two. The wait was even worse than when I'd been saving up for the Toxic Slab.

The cover of the old book Nana had given me was made from leather. It looked like Pugwash's skin – battered and scuffed, like it was hundreds of years old and had experienced many a battle.

I opened the book gently. Line after line of neatly written foreign words. They were faded but readable. I flicked through; it appeared to be a diary.

Deep in the book, a page caught my eye. There was just one single sentence in the centre of the page, surrounded with multiple black pen circles, like the writer had been intent on making a very important point. The penwork had almost carved through the page and onto the next.

This seemed like a good place to start. The words were large and clear: *Nok er nok. Vi vil stå for denne barbariteten ikke lenger!*

I picked up the small dictionary Nana Biddle had given me and took my easiest guess: this was Norwegian. I thumbed through the dictionary, trying to decipher the first few words.

I'm not the most academic person. I think that's probably obvious to you by now. This old-school-dictionary business would be no match for a techy translation solution.

Attempt 2: I took a photo of the first paragraph on my tablet and ran it through an OCR app – a handwriting-to-text converter. But it struggled with the fancy handwriting.

I googled the problem. Turned out the software needed to learn the handwriting, in real-time, to be any good.

Attempt 3: Good old-fashioned donkey work! I typed in the sentence by hand, pasted it into Translate, and *bazinga!* We had lift-off. *Enough is enough. We will stand for this barbarity no longer!*

OMG ... it had worked! The writer sounded pretty vexed. It caught my attention like an explosion. I was on a roll. I turned the page and began translating the next diary entry, paragraph by paragraph.

January 10, 1891

Det sørger meg dypt at bare i forrige uke ble jeg tilbudt ett hetteglass med trollblod til 30 krone. Tilbudet ble flatt nektet mens jeg brøt den unge gentlemanens kjeve over kneet mitt.

I hit translate … and boom. Good old English right before my eyes. I was a super spy. A super translator, unravelling the deepest secrets of the universe. Right here, right now, I was Stephen freaking Hawking!

January 10, 1891.

It saddens me that just last week I was offered one vial of troll blood for 30 krone. The offer refused while I broke the young gentleman's jaw across my knee.

Troll blood?

Holy crap. People were selling troll blood. And somebody wasn't happy about it so he'd broken the trader's jaw. This was epic … but in the way that epic can be the worst. Doc Emmett Brown would have said, 'This is heavy, Marty.' And he would have meant it in the heaviest sense of the word. I typed another paragraph into my tablet, noting, in particular, the word Månejegere.

Shrouding the clan for seven seasons we know that, at any time, we could be discovered. Should that <gibberish> we shall most certainly fall into the hands of the moon hunters but it is our Christian duty to shield the purity of the troll people [mennesker] and end their barbaric slaughter in the name of medical advancement.

Månejegere – moon hunters.

They sounded horrible.

I imagined faceless creatures with no souls – hiding in the shadows, poised to attack. Like a Boomslang snake blending into the environment, ready to strike. Shrouded in dark robes, their faces obscured … just a terrifying void with burning red eyes.

I shuddered at the darkness of my own imagination and quickly checked the window to make sure there were none outside.

I'd spooked myself, as I often did, but returned to the bed and continued typing and translating. I opened two browsers and flicked between them to speed things up.

Currently, on any occasion, all nights of the year, the night casts shadows of the moon hunters [Månejegere] slipping between the trees on the hunt. Maybe up to twenty hunting packs across just this forest region alone. I can only blame the Lovmen (those in power) for sanctioning such hunts, as the financial rewards have swollen by three since the last harvest moon and, by no coincidence, last winter's rat-flea virus (a form of plague). As the death toll rises, hysteria grips the region. There is desperation for troll blood, the only known antidote to such a <gibberish> disease. Naturally, many a young man has now fallen for the seduction of the moon hunters. This is human nature at its worst.

I couldn't believe what I was reading. It didn't matter that the odd word was gibberish – I understood perfectly! People were using troll blood as some kind of healing elixir. No wonder the poor trolls had been forced to hide. At the mercy of the Månejegere. At the mercy of greed and desperation.

I read on.

When one considers that a mature adult troll may contain up to 5,000 vials, it becomes obvious that a young forester – who may earn but 500 krone for a full season's work – can be seduced by the moon hunters for but one night's work, and earn perhaps 5,000 krone as part of a ten-man hunting pack. What life is this when the purest among society are driven to extinction by the whims of the powerful? This is man at his ugliest. This is why we, the Warriors [Krigere] must do all we can to protect the remaining trolls in our region.

I didn't know who was writing this, but I was with them one hundred million per cent. How could people be so evil?

But I knew the answer to that.

It's what *we* do. Elephants for their tusks, foxes for their fur and for sport. Those poor bulls in Spain … this is what we humans did. And it was part of the reason I didn't like the world one bit. When I'd met Forfaltrot and looked into his eyes I'd felt something amazing, like I was in the presence of the purest thing that had ever existed. I now realised why they were hiding deep underground on my grandfather's land. Troll blood was like magic, and bad men would do whatever it took, and by whatever means, to get it.

I yawned loudly. It was almost eleven and I was pretty tired, but this incredible artefact had me mesmerised.

One more paragraph. One more insight into the truth!

We must educate and find another way. The troll people must not fall victim to their own immense power and healing abilities. They are not livestock. They are not to be profiteered from. The magic in their blood that cures disease and prolongs life is not a commodity to be bought and sold. Neither must their visions of truth [sannhetens visjoner] be harnessed for ill doing by the courts of the land. A troll's wish [trollene ønsker] is not a commodity. It is a gift. And we must protect them with our lives. This is why I and Mistress Hilde [Elskerinne Hilde] are preparing to evacuate the trolls from this land. We shall sail them to England for a better life.

I turned the page and was greeted was the most incredible sight. There, before my eyes, was a photo of Nana Biddle and Dar standing by a huge lorry. They were surrounded by mountains. The photo was black and white and looked like something from the old history books. I carefully peeled the picture from the page and flipped it over.

Vi reiser i dag Januar 12, 1891

We sail today. January 12, 1891

Holy freaking crap!

There was no doubt it was them. I could have spotted my grandfather's ears anywhere. But he looked a fair bit younger. And he was hench – like bodybuilder hench. Nana Biddle was standing upright, six inches taller without her stoop.

They looked serious, determined, like a couple of badasses. Dar even had the big badass moustache. The back of the lorry was closed, but given what I'd read in the diary, I figured there was a troll, or trolls, inside.

But what truly blew my mind was the date: 1891. Nana Biddle and Dar must have been at least forty, maybe fifty years old in that photo.

But it's 2018!

That was 127 years ago.

It couldn't be right.

'That would make Dar and Nana at least 160 years old! No freaking way,' I whispered, thinking that saying the words out loud might make them more plausible. It was impossible. Just utterly, ridiculously impossible. People did *not* live that long.

But then, just a week ago, I'd thought trolls weren't real.

CHAPTER EIGHTEEN

A Step Too Far

The next morning, I woke early after another epic dream. Dad was with me. We were running through the forest, getting chased down by the men. A howling wind roared around us and we swung from tree to tree like Donkey Kong. Below us, hiding between the trees, were the Månejegere. Ancient beings, as still as the trees that shrouded them. They watched us in silence as we rode the vines, flitting from tree to tree on our own personal adventure. Dad would call out to me every so often.

'You okay, son? Keep up.'

Then he'd swing in front, encouraging me to join him at the next tree.

That's all I remember. It was one of those dreams that felt like it had played out for the whole night but was probably only a fleeting moment.

But it had been nice spending time with my dad.

I came down for breakfast, surprised to find it was just me and Wrigley waiting to be fed. I looked out of the window – horrible weather! Rain cascaded down the crooked concrete slabs and the wind was violently spinning the cockerel weathervane on top of the old barn. Not a good day to be working outside.

The kitchen table had been laid for three.

'Dar?' I called out into the hall. 'Nana?'

I became suddenly anxious, imagining all manner of terrible things that might have befallen them during the night.

'Be there soon my, little habbadehoy. Fill your own bowl.' Dar's reassuring voice came from the dining room. He was obviously dressing Nana Biddle.

I ruffled Wrigley's ears. 'Just you and me this morning, boy.'

Cornflakes, branflakes, wheatflakes, oats. Damn, with William gone, things were looking pretty bleak on the breakfast front.

The radio played to itself in the corner. The newsreader was going on about the weather. I tried to change the channel but there were no buttons, just a train-track display of numbers, a red line down the middle of the screen and a couple of big round knobs. I tried flicking the touch screen, but it didn't work. Weird old radio.

… torrential rain and strong winds could be a cause for concern if you're out and about this weekend. In terms of timing, it looks likely that Hurricane Zelda won't reach the UK until tomorrow morning across the south and east of England. It's going to be pretty blustery, especially in coastal areas. As with all red travel warnings, expect bridge closures. The Met Office is warning drivers against non-essential travel. Carla Morrison, 5 Live Weather.'

Great. Just what an indoor boy needed when he was forced outdoors. Time to get super-tech on the breakfast, too, because this growing lad required a better class of sustenance. I raided the fridge.

A couple of minutes later, Wrigley was chowing down on a tin of corned beef and I had a bowl full of *Brandon Mess* – like Eton Mess except my marvellous concoction was a big bowl of yoghurt and maple syrup with smashed up flapjack and Crunchie bar.

Muscle food!

My grandparents came in. Nana hummed cheerily and kissed my cheek as she passed, while Dar throttled me playfully when he saw my marvellous creation.

'You'll do yourself a mischief with all that sugary slop, boy.'

'Meh,' I said, shrugging it off as I drained the last dregs of syrup directly into my mouth.

I was biding my time this morning. There were so many more questions to ask but I wasn't sure what I should or shouldn't say in front of Nana Biddle.

Dar bought a rack of steaming toast to the table and wrestled with Wrigley while he fought to get his morning kiss. It was something I just couldn't get used to as it involved a considerable amount of dog growling, floor scratching, jumping and slobber all over Dar's face and beard. Dar was a man of routine, however, and I loved the way he loved his dog – like I loved my fat, useless cat.

I destroyed the last of my *Brandon Mess* and began nibbling on a slice of toast and honey – watching Dar and Nana Biddle slurp on hot porridge. I was biding my time today, waiting for the perfect opportunity …

'Dar.'

'Yes, boy.'

'Is Nana demented … has she got, you know, dementia?'

Dar paused, his full spoon hanging in mid-air. 'Don't be so bloody rude.'

I waited for the porridge to fall off, but it didn't. Dar's porridge would have been better off in Wickes as brick cement.

'Your grandmother's sitting right across the table.'

'Sorry, Dar.'

'To your grandmother!' Dar snapped.

'Sorry, Nana.'

Nana Biddle looked at me, her eyes loaded with curiosity.

'Why do you ask?' Dar didn't look at me, just pulled his newspaper across the table and untangled the chain on his reading glasses.

'Just because.'

Dar hmm'd and opened the paper, flicking immediately to the obituary page – a section I've learned is quite important to old people as it tells them who's died recently … like an elderly person's Top Trumps.

'How old are you, Nana?'

She smiled, sneaked a glance at Dar, and pulled her cardigan tight around her chest.

'You know it's impolite to ask a lady her age, boy,' Dar snapped.

I put my hand over Nana Biddle's and squeezed. 'Love you, Nan.' And helped myself to another slice of toast.

'How old are you then, Dar? If it's only rude to ask a lady.'

'As old as my hair and a little older than my teeth,' he said, shovelling a loaded spoon of porridge into his mouth. Though most of it spilled onto his straggly grey beard.

'Ha, ha, ha, donk. That's my head falling on the floor coz you're just so funny.' I nibbled around the crust, getting rid of the unbuttered bits. Ready for the best part.

'Tell you what. You guess my age. If you're wrong, you get to help Pugwash shovel up the chicken-crap. But if you're correct, you get a prize. A fart-catcher's day off. Three guesses decide the outcome.'

Dar stirred a heap of sparrow food onto his porridge and shook the empty syrup bottle.

'Shame we don't have any maple syrup!' He threw the plastic bottle at my head playfully. I parried it onto the floor like a ninja. Wrigley went mental on it as the bottle shot across the tiles, gnashing it between his teeth, throwing his head from side to side like a crocodile in full-on attack mode. Growling and ripping it to pieces with his claws. The stupid mutt was obviously high on sugar.

'Are you sixty-three?'

'Nope!'

'Higher or lower?'

'Lower!'

'Funny. Are you four hundred and twenty-two?'

'Steady, boy, or you'll be for another face-full of chicken muck.'

I sucked in a deep breath and went for it. 'You were born sometime in the mid eighteen-hundreds.' I paused, waiting for a reaction, but there was nothing. 'So that makes you about a hundred and sixty years old.'

Dar placed his spoon carefully in his bowl and Nana Biddle did a little choke on her porridge.

'Does it now?' Dar dabbed at his mouth with a napkin.

'Yes it does. And I also know that you and Nana sailed across from Norway in 1891! With a lorry of full of trolls.'

Dar took a gargantuan slurp of tea and slammed his cup down on the table. He rose and loomed over Nana Biddle.

'You stupid, *stupid* woman. And you,' – Dar pointed angrily into my face – 'there's to be no more talk of trolls, Pitchbury Wood, anything again. *Ever.*'

He was shaking with anger, like when I'd pushed him towards the forest with William.

'Goddamn you, woman. Do you want the boy to lose his tongue too?'

I'd never seen anyone so angry. Ever. It was even worse than when Aayush had put fart powder in his Uncle's Tarka dhal.

'Am I to be understood?'

I didn't answer so Dar slammed the kitchen table with both palms.

'*DO YOU UNDERSTAND ME?*

'Yes, I understand,' I said in my littlest voice.

Dar stormed out of the room. Wrigley followed, wagging his tail. A few moments later there was a loud yelp and the old dog skulked back into the kitchen and hid under the table. Nana Biddle rose timidly, placed her arm around my shoulder and kissed me gently on the cheek.

'I'm sorry, Nana.'

She squeezed me close and brushed my cheek with her own. She smelled of old soap and her whiskers tickled my nose. If I were being polite I might have said that Nana Biddle had an invisible beard, but in truth it wasn't particularly invisible at all.

She picked up the sugar bowl and tipped the contents into the centre of the table, then spread it with her palm, creating a sugary desert.

Then she traced her finger through it.

He is full of fear.

Nana drew a heart underneath it and crossed the 'I' with a kiss. She cradled my face and opened her mouth several times as if to speak, but all that came out were horrible moans.

She rubbed her palm across the sugary desert, creating a blank canvas, then traced her finger once again.

'Great danger.'

The back door slammed and we both watched Dar, dressed in his tatty raincoat – the one with the straw bale string belt – leaning into the wind as he hobbled down the yard on his crutches.

'I read the book, Nana. I know about you leaving Norway with the trolls. I know about the trollblod, the Månejegere. I know it all. It's okay, Nana. I know.'

She rubbed out the sugar words and rested her trembling finger. She wrote a few letters, scribbled them out. Tried again but erased them too.

'What, Nana? You can tell me. What danger?'

Nana pushed the sugar into her porridge bowl and trudged across the kitchen to the bin.

'You can tell me, Nana. How? How are we in danger?'

She returned to her chair, slumped down wearily and looked at me across the table. There was so much sadness in her eyes.

Then she lowered her head and sat like a statue – gently humming an unknown song.

CHAPTER NINETEEN

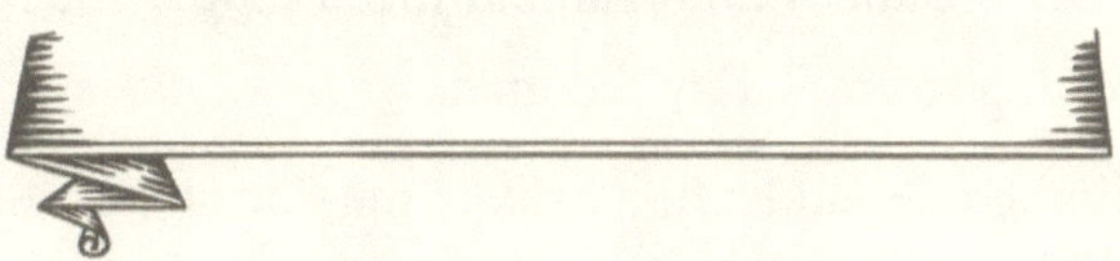

The Darkest Truths

Later that morning, after checking a bazillion times for Aayush's email, I went to find Dar.

The rain was forcing little muddy rivers to cascade down the yard. I decided to wear two T-shirts under a hoodie and my winter coat to keep the weather on the outside and me warm on the inside. The storm was certainly on its way; the tops of the trees rocked with every angry gust of wind.

'Dar, where are you?' I shouted down the yard, my voice losing its battle to be heard.

I sheltered in the doorway of the old calving shed – the building they used to raise the baby cows.

I listened hard and heard a faint but faint banging of hammer against metal.

I ran down the yard, hugging the buildings to shelter from the rain, jumping over puddles and brown streams to protect my trainers. I'd worn the wellington boots Dar had given me once – on the day he'd bought them – so as not to seem ungrateful, but, really, for a town kid wellies were just not okay!

Dar was up top of the old milking parlour, possibly the most run-down building on the entire farm. Only a farmer would risk life and limb on an old metal roof in the middle of a brewing storm. Crazy old man.

I climbed the ladder he'd fixed to the side of the building. Carefully, so as not to slip.

'Can I help?' I knelt next to Dar and took hold of the edge of the large sheet of aluminium that threatened to lift him into the sky with every gust.

'You shouldn't be up here!' Dar's tone suggested his anger was still front and centre.

'And neither should you. But the job'll be finished sooner with two pairs of hands.'

I put my knee on the metal sheet. Dar banged a screw into place, then fixed it with a weird drill he had to turn by hand.

We mended the parlour roof in silence. Then I helped Dar carry the tools down the ladder and back to the toolshed.

Once inside, Dar lit the old wood burner and placed a kettle on top.

'Ovaltine and rum?' He warmed his hands over the stove, waggling his fingers like a magician as the kettle began to steam.

'Sure,' I replied, wondering why my grandfather was offering me hard alcohol.

Dar left the toolshed and disappeared into the house.

I waited.

And waited.

The kettle came to the boil and started to whistle. It was awesome. I hadn't known such things even existed – a kettle that didn't need electricity and told you when it was ready. I wondered if it was Bluetooth … but doubted it – Dar didn't have a mobile or tablet. It was probably the most technological thing he possessed.

I took the kettle off the stove and went to find him in the house.

His voice was raised and sharp. I tiptoed across the hall.

'You had no right … We're supposed to be protecting him! From danger, from the ugliness. It's a heavy weight, Hilde. He needs to know all he needs to know … and not an iota more. No child should have to carry that kind of darkness.'

I peeked into the kitchen. Dar stood over Nana, who sat unmoving at the table. He used the Ovaltine jar to emphasise his point.

'You had no right, Hilde. He's just a child.'

I stormed into the kitchen, determined to protect Nana Biddle from an unjust rollocking.

'I wasn't a child when I saved you from the quad crash and I certainly wasn't a child when I got rid of Councillor Lackshaft in the top field. So make your damn mind up! Don't have a go at Nana. She didn't do anything wrong, for Christ's sake.' My anger had pushed my bravery bar a little higher today. Dar was out of order and needed telling. 'You can't just pick and choose when I'm allowed to be involved. You showed me, Dar – the trolls, William's stories, the chicken mission. So shout at me, Dar. Not Nana. Me!'

Dar grabbed my coat collar and dragged me on the tips of my toes back to the toolshed. He didn't even bother with his crutches – just pure, unaided Dar power. He tossed me roughly onto the workbench, where I slumped in shock and disbelief.

He stormed across the toolshed, opened a little cubbyhole and pulled out a cardboard box. Blowing off the dust, he slammed it onto the workbench next to me and nodded towards it. Dragon fire danced in his eyes.

'You want to know about right and wrong, boy? There!'

I stared at the box, terrified by what might be inside.

'OPEN IT!'

I pulled out what looked like a large, rusty metal pair of shark jaws. I knew what it was as I'd used something similar on *Survarium* – a survival game on the PC – to catch my enemies.

I raised my head, confused and fearful of what I might see in his rage-filled eyes. I inspected the device. It was heavy; and it didn't budge a millimetre when I tried to prise it open.

'It's a bear trap,' I said timidly.

'It's a troll trap!' Dar said, his eyes heavy with unspeakable sadness.

Holding a real trap was a whole different ballgame from using one in a made-up RPG. I dropped the device back into the box. It was horrific; thinking of what it might do to a living creature almost brought me to tears.

'The weapon of choice for the Månejegere. Because a *dead* troll is of no value.' Dar hissed the words through gritted teeth; not angry anymore – just … I dunno … hurt maybe? It was hard to listen to.

I folded the flaps of the box in on each other, hoping I might somehow be able to un-see this horrific contraption.

'When a troll dies the blood turns dark … and dark troll blood is a deadly toxin.'

'Why are you showing me this?' My bones itched with disgust and I suddenly wished I'd never been shown, or told, anything.

'Because, as angry as I am with Hilde, you have a right to know the danger you're in.'

'I'm not stupid, Dar. I get it!' I snapped, desperate to show him I wasn't the stupid little kid he thought I was. 'You're scared. And I know all about that. I'm scared every single day I walk into school. Every minute of every day I'm waiting for the next attack. So, yeah, I get how you feel. I've got my bully and you've got yours.'

Dar pushed the box back into the cubbyhole and covered it with a dirty sack. Then he grabbed a couple of cups from a shelf and poured in the steaming water.

'You asked me to explain when we were fixing the chicken fence. I cry myself to sleep most nights because I'm terrified of a bully I can't stop. A horrible, evil, spiteful prick of a boy called *Aiden Hunt*. And to really twist the knife, he's the boy of my dad's soon-to-be wife. He's at school, he's on the internet, Snapchat, everywhere. Do you have any idea what it's like to go to sleep every night and somewhere, deep inside, not care whether you wake up or not?'

Dar stirred the cups in silence.

Dar sighed deeply. 'I have to protect you.' He scooped a couple of spoons of chocolate Ovaltine into each cup and pulled a small bottle of rum from his jacket pocket.

A glug in each cup was followed by a quick whisk of the spoon.

'Well, nobody has so far, Dar, and it seems to me like you're on your own here too … on the farm, fighting a fight you've no chance of winning. I hurt, Dar, every minute of every day, and it's not until I came here that you showed me something I can believe in. So I'm sorry I went behind your back and delved deeper into your life. But I want to help. I need to help. And maybe by helping you, I can find a way to help myself along the way. I just don't want to hurt anymore. I don't want to be scared anymore, Dar. How can that be so bad?'

Dar passed me the cup. 'Oh, my dear little habbadehoy … when did you get so grown-up?'

I cradled the choco-rum in my palms, feeling the warmth and taking comfort from it.

'I see so much of myself in you.' Dar sipped his drink and seemed to chill a little. 'I know about pain too. A long time ago I put my trust in someone and it brought them great danger. I hurt the one I loved the most by selfishly sharing my burden with them. I nearly lost everything, Brandon. Everything I hold dear … everything that matters to me. We all have our bullies, boy. But sometimes the greater war is won through compassion. Through patience and waiting. And then we hope … and we pray. And maybe, just maybe, that's enough to keep the ones we hold dearest from immediate danger.'

I crossed my legs and looked through the toolshed window. Columns of autumn leaves swirled like mini tornados. A pair of magpies fought to stay upright in the birch hedge. It was truly horrible out there.

'As long as you're under my roof, I'm responsible for you. And I *will not* risk your safety any more than I already have. Regardless of how ready or how obligated you feel to join our battle.'

'But I already knew, didn't I? So what if Nana filled in a few blanks. I'm either a Kriger or I'm not. Like you said, I'm not a little kid anymore. Besides, you're the one who showed me. You're the one who took me to meet them. And you are *really* old. And I'm ready to step up.'

'I can't do it, Brandon. This isn't a game.' Dar sipped his hot choco-rum and stared deep into my eyes. 'You don't get another life or level up.' Dar softened. 'I'm worried I can't protect you. And the more you know, the worse the danger.'

'I know. And I'm sorry. But I've seen what's happening here. I totally understand what we need to do, Dar. We can't let Lackshaft push us around anymore. It's not healthy. And I just want to be here for you both.' Warily, I threw out a timid question … 'I'm sorry but I just absolutely have to know. Are you really that old?'

Dar snapped a couple of sticks and tossed them into the wood burner. The orange flames danced as if to show their gratitude.

'*Pah!* What's age anyway? It's how you feel, right? It's how you feel in here.' Dar patted his chest. 'And in here.' He tapped his head.

I clearly wasn't going to get a straight answer so changed my approach.

'Does Lackshaft know everything? There must be a way we can get him out of our faces.'

'He likes to think he does. Enough to be extremely dangerous, that's for certain. He knows enough to take fresh interest in our land, and that's not to be underestimated.' Dar opened the toolshed door and glanced outside. The wind howled and the rain lashed sideways, the water ricocheting up as it met the ground.

'Are they Månejegere?' I asked, as Dar forced the door shut and returned to my side.

Dar sighed again. He was sighing a lot today!

'Not going to shut up till you get your answers, are you?'

I shook my head.

'A century ago, yes. But now they're government officials, part of the second estate envoy. Councillors, civil servants, ministers, delegates. Fancy names to hide behind and draw influence from. Just as dangerous but carrying the full weight of the law.'

Dar refilled our cups and hopped onto the counter next to me.

It was certainly a calming brew. My new favourite hot drink.

'So they're after you and Nana because they know you've got the trolls. Because they know you smuggled them to safety, right?'

'And they'll *never* stop,' Dar said, his voice cracking.

I didn't know how to deal with it other than patting his arm and saying something nice.

'You risk your lives for them. Every day. Like modern-day heroes. Like those soldiers we see in town with the metal legs.' I nudged my shoulder into his. 'I love you, Dar!'

That caught him off guard, but I saw in his eyes that he felt it too.

'Imagine this, my little habbadehoy. Imagine what'd become of the pharmaceutical industry if all man-made medicines were suddenly obsolete. Cancer, heart disease, illnesses of the blood, bone and mind ... suddenly curable. Chemotherapy, dialysis, blood transfusions, transplants. Obsolete. The world economy would collapse. Whether Lackshaft wants to control the farming of troll blood for his own wealth, or he's working on behalf of the pharmaceutical companies to eliminate the risk, I don't know ... and I truly don't care. Either way it's a despicable outcome. Yet another war of greed waged against innocence.'

I shuffled closer, mesmerised.

'Please, Dar, don't stop. I need to understand.'

'The year Nana and I left Norway, troll farming began. Intensive farming. Trapping and herding. Caged like battery hens, chained up with little room to move. Force-fed just enough to keep drawing breath. Blood-letting twice, three times a day.'

Dar hopped down from the bench and stoked the fire, wiggling an iron spike into the heart of the embers to bring the flames back to life.

'A production line of troll blood, a magical cure-all for the rich and influential. And then, once the troll was spent, death!'

He swept a pile of sawdust from the worktop and onto the floor, then picked out a couple of screws and dropped them into an old metal coffee jar. He grabbed a hunk of chalk and expertly tossed it into a rusty old paint pot on the other side of the toolshed. I copied him, grabbing a smaller chunk and trying to repeat the slam dunk. Missed!

'That was about the time the stories began. *Fee, fi, fo, fum. I smell the blood of a Christian man. Be he alive or be he dead, I'll grind his bones to make my bread.*' Dar paced around the centre of the toolshed, theatrically stamping his feet, sadness etched across the furrows in his elderly face.

'If only people had known. But they were full of fear after the hideous propaganda. Folk were dropping like flies from the rat-flea virus and they were prepared to believe anything. It was such a terrible time. Such a terrible, terrible time.'

I felt the tears stream down my face and was powerless to stop them. I didn't want to hear anymore and yet I didn't want him to stop either. Dar hopped back up next to me and pulled me close.

'Weighs heavily, doesn't it?'

I nodded, wiping the tears away with my sleeve.

'Trolls don't turn to stone, lurk under bridges, or chase villagers from their homes. They're a peaceful race. Gifted tribal folk, fjellhelbrederen – the healers from the mountain. Used. Killed. Burned. Then left where they could be found to fuel the propaganda. That, my boy, is the truth of a troll.'

Dar bum-shuffled across the countertop and collected a small metal box. He rummaged inside and pulled out a tiny package wrapped in several layers of brown paper. Each one was carefully removed, unveiling a metal badge. He tossed it to me.

I held it up to the light. A golden lion holding an axe, and above that, also in gold, the words Til Fred. Dar shuffled back, took the badge from my hand and pinned it onto my coat. He took a deep breath and tugged on his beard.

I rubbed the badge with my sleeve, bringing a shine back to it 'The same inscription as on Snaghorn, Dar.'

'It means until peace. And if a person, such as Nana or myself, the trollfolk Krigere – warriors of the troll people – must die to save a troll, then that, my little habbadehoy, is the way it's meant to be. For if my life were to end tomorrow, I would take my last breath with pride, knowing I was one of the last remaining Krigere. Because that's what we are … and now, you also. We are Kriger. Warriors of the troll people! But we don't go off gung-ho. This is the real world. This is life or death. This is war. And besides, I owe it to your mother to keep that lovely face of yours intact. One day you'll be a man … and you will be ready. Now, come on. Give your old Dar a hug.'

I cuddled into my grandfather and glanced down at the badge, now knowing the full extent of the weight it carried. I wasn't scared or even remotely anxious.

Dar was wrong though.

I was ready.

I was Kriger, a chosen warrior for the troll people.

And if my life were to end tomorrow, I too would take my last breath with nothing but pride.

CHAPTER TWENTY

An Act of Treason

I returned to the house and checked in on Nana Biddle. She was in her bedroom, cleaning her teeth. Which meant she was holding them in her hand. Truly gross.

I ran up the stairs two at a time and locked myself in the bedroom. The books I'd left laid out on the bed had been moved! As had my tablet. After a quick inspection, I found the Toxic Slab in the drawer, but the books were nowhere to be found. Oh well, they'd served their purpose and I knew all I needed, now that Dar had filled in the rest.

The Toxic Slab powered up like a rocket. YES! And there was an email from Aayush.

I stuffed a whole KitKat into my mouth and army-rolled onto the bed. I was back in the game.

The audio file copied across to my phone in a blink. It took only a couple of minutes for the translation software to install, just enough time to queue up the audio file on my tablet.

The last ten per cent of the installation took ages but then it was ready!

I tapped the icon on my phone. An orange glow washed across the hub screen and I selected my input language, Norwegian, and my output language, English.

My trembling finger hovered over the big orange translate button. I tapped my finger, held, then pressed Play.

And there it was, the magic, playing through my tablet speakers.

Forfaltrot's gruff, bellowy voice was instantly recognisable.

'Without help, what meaning to life,' came the computerised translation. 'Small price for peace and sanctuary.'

I replayed the voice clip multiple times, laughing out loud from the buzz. I was the troll whisperer. I was Doctor Who with my sonic screwdriver, though not the latest lady one! Mage. Wizard. Word sorcerer.

A badass Kriger super spy!

I almost fell downstairs in my rush to find Dar as I straddled the carpeted steps and used the painted skirting board to ski, Eddie the Eagle style, to the bottom. A much better way to use stairs … though absolutely forbidden, of course.

Dar was on the cottage cheese again. Or I should say, his beard was. He sat at the table, studying the newspaper.

I plonked my butt down opposite him, full of beans, impatient to show him my amazing findings.

'Dar, check this out!'

'In a moment,' he said. He traced his finger across the text – *Worst storm in decades.* More fearmongering about the weather.

'Dar, it's awesome. Look!'

Dar shushed me and continued to read the paper. It was torture! I bounced in the chair, desperate to share my findings with him, but there was no budging him.

Eventually, he looked up, closed the paper and folded it neatly on the table.

Finally, I had his attention.

'Get ready to be blown away, Dar. This is chicken oriental mental. Ready?'

He continued munching, clearly not sharing my enthusiasm. So I casually hit the Translate button and pressed play.

Prepare to have your mind blown – old man!

Forfaltrot's awesome foreign voice filled the room. Then, a moment later, came the digital translation.

Dar stopped munching.

'It's Forfaltrot! He's happy. He's grateful,' I said, waiting for Dar to clasp his hands over his mouth with awe and profess how incredibly clever I was. Dar just nodded and scooped a big blob of cheese onto a cracker.

'Awesome, isn't it? I recorded his voice when we went under the forest. Then I got Aayush to stealth his dad's new translator app,' I said, leaning into Dar and counting off the genius achievements on my fingers.

'I slowed the audio down on my video software, so the app would understand it. And bish-bash-bosh, a talking troll.'

I placed my tablet and phone on the table.

'It's a talking troll, Dar! I deciphered it. We can find out anything now. All the amazing secrets from the past. We can know it all.'

Dar finished his mouthful. 'A clever feat indeed.' His enthusiasm was a million miles away from my own.

'I'm going to wrap up warm, run back later and give Nana's dolls to the troll twins. I've got so many questions to ask, Dar.'

I jumped up and circled the table, my turbo brain coming up with all manner of possibilities.

'Do you reckon they have super powers? I'll just ask. Like laser vision or teleportation. Real-life Hulk-smash abilities. Like when he rescued us and whooshed the quad-bike through the hedge. I wonder how high they can jump. Clean over the house maybe. Maybe they can fly. I'll just ask. Simples!'

Dar swept the crumbs onto his plate and took it across to the sink, then finished his lunch with a small glass of water.

'What will you ask, Dar? I want to know what it was like back in Norway when the brown stuff was hitting the fan. Do you think they fought like warriors, smashing up the bad guys and their trucks with huge trees they'd just ripped from the ground?'

I mimed out the action around the kitchen, using the paper-towel pole as a prop.

'Settle down, boy. You'll give yourself an aneurism.' Dar grabbed my sleeve and dragged me back into my seat. 'You'll give *me* an aneurism. I can't think straight with all this boisterousness. Listen!' He pulled up the chair next to me. 'You can't just go riding out into the storm. You know that. There are eyes everywhere now, and things need to settle. Sure, Lackshaft's gone for now, and that's down to your wits, but he will be back. We bide our time … and wait it out. Get through winter.'

Dar was calm and composed. Dull. Old and dull. Not the Kriger I'd pledged my life to fight alongside.

He picked up the broom and began sweeping the floor. I watched, mortified, as my warrior grandfather chose such a timid activity in the midst of my rallying battle cry.

'Come on, Dar – we're Krigere!' I took the broom from his hands and placed it back in the corner. 'You won't have the farm by then. Lackshaft will have stolen it from you, and we can't let that happen, right? We're warriors!' I fixed him with my most serious, bravery-filled glare. 'We're warriors, Dar. And warriors don't wait. They fight!'

My grandfather recovered the broom and continued sweeping, taking great care to get into the corners.

'No. I've made my decision. I forbid it.'

I stared at him, rapidly losing respect for him.

'So you're just an old coward then?'

Dar stopped and settled the broom against the counter.

'What did you call me?'

'I asked. I didn't call. I asked if you were a coward. The Dar in the toolshed earlier spoke like a Kriger. And now you just want to sweep the floor and wait till the weather gets a bit warmer. Won't Lackshaft have taken away the farm by then? We'll have nothing!'

'My wife …' – Dar's voice rattled with emotion – 'your grandmother, lost her tongue to a blade the last time I made a rash decision. Grow up! You dare to imply I'm a coward for making conservative decisions to protect my own. That's the problem with your generation – no long-term thought. You think in your twelve years on this planet you've got it all worked out, do you?' Dar was rattled. I could tell from the way his knuckles had gone white as he gripped the broom. 'Rash decisions cost lives. You could live a thousand lifetimes and not scratch the surface of what I've seen with these eyes. There's an innocence in you, Brandon. And I intend to keep it that way. I admire your will to help, but please, out of respect to your grandmother and I, let things be. One day, you'll be ready.'

He turned the broom on its side to get at the cobwebs on the skirting boards.

'So what's the plan?' I was aching with anticipation to hear more about the long game he was trying to sink into my stupid young head. I shifted my weight from one foot to the other as Dar concentrated on getting every last spiderweb from the corners of the kitchen floor.

'I don't know,' he muttered into his chest.

I stared, as he struggled to kneel and sweep the rubbish into a dustpan. He clambered to his feet, then emptied the dirt and crap into the bin.

And then I just walked away.

There was a mission to complete and Dar's over-cautious nature was most certainly not going to crush my plans.

Later that evening, I lay on my bed, still as a corpse. I regulated my breathing and worked on keeping my mind still and calm. Rational thoughts; good thoughts that would help not hinder. There was no room for uncertainty tonight. Unlike Dar, I was focused. Filled with positive energy.

Something *had* changed in me. The little boy so full of fear had died the night we crashed the quad. Yeah, I was still scared about things, but I rose above my fear, remembering what Dar had taught me about heroes.

A hero is not a person without fear, but someone who does what's right in spite of it.

And then Rocky Balboa came to mind:

You, me, or nobody is gonna hit as hard as life. But it ain't about how hard ya hit. It's about how hard you can get hit and keep moving forward. How much you can take and keep moving forward. That's how winning is done!

I'd memorised that speech from start to finish. Watched it over and over before and after school a million times. But it never seemed to embed itself in my bravery motherboard.

Aiden Hunt could only win if I let him. Lackshaft would only win if we let him.

I, we, were stronger.

I hadn't thought about *Aiden Hunt* since Lackshaft's first visit.

'Aiden Hunt.' I spoke his name slowly and deliberately. And for the first time in ever it didn't make my stomach lurch. That sense of dread didn't drag itself from my heart to my throat. I wasn't scared anymore, and the day I returned to school I'd prove it to him.

As for Dar, I'd lost faith in him. He preached well, but when it came to the shove he'd rather sweep the kitchen floor. I wanted to race into his room, drag him out of his fusty old chair by the ears and shake some courage into him. He might be prepared to wait until winter had passed and hope for the best, but I wasn't.

I breathed in through my nose, out through my mouth. *Steady mind. Steady hand. Sturdy heart.* My new mantra. I said the words to myself between every breath.

The shrill phone alarm broke the silence, rudely snapping me out of my meditation.

I was the Kriger now. And it was time to prove it. To my grandparents … but most importantly, to myself.

The wind took my breath away and the rain slashed my face like icy razors. Nature as ferocious as I could imagine. I clung to the corner of the farmhouse, hugging the wall, staring across the yard at my next micro destination. I was forced back on my heels, my body threatening to become a kite as a distant, growling rumble of thunder reminded me of my insignificance. Pulling my jumper over my nose, I prepared to fight my way into the stormy night.

I took a bold step forward.

The security light on the corner of the farmhouse glowed to life. Several guinea fowl in the chicken paddock began squawking and I froze. I checked my phone. Ten past nine. By now, Dar would have settled Nana Biddle and be supping on his evening brew, feet up and watching the news. He'd be oblivious.

I waited for a moment then dashed across the yard, amazed by the power of the wind as it taunted me and tried to force me back to the safety of the farmhouse.

Go home, little boy. Whooo do you think yoou aaare?

Taking cover in the shadow of the birch hedge, I plotted my next move. I took a series of deep, calming breaths.

Then I ran across the yard and through the barn. The huge door almost chopped me in half as it smashed open and shut in the ferocious wind.

A sprint to the parlour, a climb through the fence into the orchard, and I was out and heading for Flossy's Field.

The wind and rain licked my cheeks like burning electrical whips. But it was tolerable. The weather laughed at me – whispering through the trees: *Run Brandon … Freeze … Run … Run freeeeee.* The treetops swayed to the rhythm, guiding me forward with their song of encouragement. Reminding me I was brave.

And then, by the old oak at the corner of the orchard, I took a moment to compose myself and catch my breath.

Turn back … Run home.

The branches above mocked my stupidity for daring to believe. For daring to find courage enough for this ridiculous wind-and-rain-swept mission.

I looked back towards the farm and saw the warm light of my bedroom window. A comforting beacon to home in on if it all became too much.

I could turn back now, tuck myself into bed and wait it out until after the winter. I was just a kid after all. Besides, it was dark here in the country, devoid of the warm bathing light from the streetlamps. I must have been stupid to think I could go it alone, into the night where God knows what might be waiting for me.

I checked under my jacket, ensuring the dolls were tucked safely inside, and suddenly felt foolish for even daring to think I could embark on such a hellish mission.

That's it, child … see sense … run along home.

The wind knew I was out of my depth and delighted in telling me so. I was defeated before I'd even begun. The scared kid who hid in the art-class cupboard, the boy who cuddled his little brother tight at night because he didn't want to feel so alone. The lad on the windowsill, sitting back as his elderly grandfather had his life torn apart.

I checked my phone; the light felt warm on my face. 9.20 p.m. A message from an unknown number.

Think you can block me that easy? I'll C U at School, Ballard. We'll be waiting! U pikey prick!!!

Aiden Hunt.

Aiden Hunt.

AIDEN HUNT.

No.

I slid the phone back into my pocket, zipped it tight, and took a bold step forward. Then another. And then another.

Then I was running. Under the barbed wire. A strong jump across the ditch. And into the open space of the top field. Ever closer to my destination in the heart of Pitchbury Wood.

AIDEN HUNT. The wind roared.

AAAAAAAAIDEN HUUUUNT!

I let the storm guide me as my legs and arms pumped me forward. Every sinew in my body willed me onward to the rallying cry of the gale.

Out in the open, the wind was a different beast. Fierce and unrelenting – battering me from all angles. I leant in and pushed on. Lightning flashed, illuminating the whole of Pitchbury Wood on the horizon. Deep, mournful thunder rumbled across the sky a second later. I willed my adrenaline to drive me forward, the name of my tormentor rolling through my head like a drum.

I would be a victim no longer.

It ain't about how hard ya hit. It's about how hard you can get hit and keep moving forward. How much you can take and keep moving forward. That's how winning is done!

The wind bellowed into my back. *Run, Kriger. Run.*

I tucked my arms in to stabilise myself and made my final dash for the trees. A mini-marathon, the wind on my back lending a hand to the child warrior on his perilous mission. I just hoped I could remember the path into the forest, winding from the break in the fence to the huge old oak.

I ate up the ground, fuelled by adrenaline, hatred, anger, fear.

And the Kriger blood flowing through my veins.

I powered through, cheered on by every swell of wind and explosive clap of thunder.

Run child. Brave, child.

I vaulted the broken fence and entered Pitchbury Wood. Then, desperate to get my bearings in the brutal darkness, I froze.

The forest was a different entity in the black of night, and, boy, could I feel it. The air was thick, closing in all around me. Choking me with its dark energy. And I suddenly felt terrified.

I imagined the Månejegere. Faceless brutes with piercing red eyes, lurking in the shadows. Coiled to attack.

My breath hung in front of my face, and every step and snap of twig echoed through the trees, stripping away my courage as I imagined a thousand eyes locked onto me.

It wasn't raining inside Pitchbury Wood; the thick canopy somehow deflected the wind and rain like a magical forcefield. I took cover under every tree, using the tricks of the Månejegere to blend into my environment.

Because I had to push on. Dar, Nana, the trolls all depended on me now. This was my chance to yell in the face of my fears.

The boy, no more. Fear gone.

I was relieved to locate the tortured tree stump, the one Dar told me had been hit by lightning and served as a reminder of nature's greatest power. I hoped I wouldn't suffer the same fate as the sky flashed and another rumble of thunder mocked me through the trees.

I stumbled blindly through a patch of brambles and then, amazingly, was in the clearing, standing under the huge oak. I crouched down under it, catching my breath.

'HELLO?'

I pulled the bag with the dolls in it from under my coat, overjoyed that it hadn't fallen out as I'd Usain Bolted across the field.

'HELLO? Forfaltrot, it's me, Brandon!' My voice ripped through the trees, disturbing a couple of pheasants who noisily broke cover – almost making me crap my pants.

I crept over to the small mounded entrance to trolldom.

'It's me, Brandon! Are you there?'

Nothing.

I squatted down and waited. The forest lit up and I counted: One elephant … two elephant … three elephant.

The thunder cracked. But still no answer. No rising of the mound. No trolls responding to my call.

I still had one trick up my sleeve. I unscrewed the lid of one of Nana Biddle's honeypots, placed it next to the mound and scurried back to my waiting spot.

Two more lightning strikes.

Still no trolls.

I searched for a latch, a doorbell, a mailbox … anything, then realised it was utterly ridiculous to imagine a postman trekking out to the woods to deliver troll mail.

Where the hell were they?

I placed the doll bag beside the honey, next to the mound, and stamped hard on the earth.

'Forfaltrot, it's me, Brandon. Please let me in,' I shouted, hoping my voice might project through the earth and sting a troll's ear.

Still nothing.

Another wash of blinding light was followed by a huge clap of thunder. This time it revealed a shadow between the trees. Not a troll shadow. A person shadow. Official, upright, suited. Standing twenty metres away and staring in my direction.

It held its hand out to me slowly.

Freaking me right out.

'HERE, BOY!' The voice ripped through the wind and I froze on the spot. 'DON'T BE SCARED!'

Another flash of lightning revealed more of the man. His face was washed out from the shadow of a large hood.

I hunched into the space at the base of the tree, trying to telepathically project my urgency into the ground. *Please let me in. I'm not brave anymore. Please.*

The ground seemed to creak and the mound lifted ever so slightly. A huge eye greeted me, and an almighty hand reached out. It grabbed the doll bag and dragged it under the forest floor. Gripped with fear, I flicked the honeypot into the hole and stared at Forfaltrot.

I looked back into the forest. Into the darkness.

The troll reached out and touched my hand. And then my mind was filled with love … and his words, as if they'd been spoken directly into my ear.

Run home, Kriger. Let wind nor rain nor evil slow your stride. Run, and don't look back. Go!

He released my hand and I watched it retreat into the ground. The cave opening re-fused with the forest floor. A blink ago, a portal to trolldom. Now nothing more than earth and twigs.

I sprang to my feet and ran. Through the brambles and the fence. Into the field, where the wind and rain were ready to meet me. Forcing every breath back into my face.

I dropped my head and powered through.

A flash of cripplingly bright white light. A crash of thunder.

I stopped and stared back at the forest. The silhouette of a man was sprinting towards me across the field. Big, powerful and gaining on me with each and every adult stride.

The wind and rain guided me forward.

Runnnn warrior, runnnn like the windddd …

I dug deep. Summoned all the warrior, all the Kriger, all the courage inside, and sprinted towards the corner of the field where the old oak tree met the orchard.

The light from my bedroom glowed faintly in the distance. My beacon.

Run warrior, run like the wind …

I reached the muddy track and the fence that divided Flossy's Field from the orchard. My hand met the barbed wire fence, ready to vault.

I felt a wallop.

I was hit.

Knocked into the mud.

The man. His hands all over me, grabbing me, wrestling me to my feet.

'Hold still, you little bastard!' His free hand fumbled with a walkie-talkie. 'I've got him, sir. The chicken is in the coop.'

I thrashed and shrieked but my cries for help were lost to the wind.

'Don't fight it, young-un. Calm your boots.'

This was not how it was going to end. I would *not* prove Dar right. I'd not be the kid who'd given the game away. The child among men.

I rolled and twisted with every ounce of my remaining strength, trying to be a crocodile in a death roll. But the man was so strong. He lifted me to my feet. Bright torchlight was shined in my eyes.

'What have we here then? Hello, boy.' I recognised the moustache. That huge squirrel moustache. Lackshaft's man. The one from the helicopter.

I wriggled madly – the wet mud and rain made it difficult for him to keep his grip on me. Lifting my legs, I pushed hard against a fence post, sending the man toppling backwards into the mud. I grabbed his torch and smashed it across Squirrel Moustache's head.

Yes! I was free.

I skidded across the track and dived into the ditch, not waiting to see whether I'd knocked him out or split his head in half – like Fruit Ninja.

Waist-deep in ditch water, shallow enough to crawl through, I dragged myself away. My body was on fire with adrenaline. Fighting. Flighting.

All I could hear was the wind, the rain, and my pulse pounding against the walls of my skull as I belly-crawled through the bottom of the ditch – a hellhole of brambles and thorns. Whipping. Ripping. Taunting me for my decision to hide in the slurry and run-off rainwater.

It was hard-going, but my motivation was strong. Helped by the crackling of two-way radios as the men closed in on me. Heightened by the dancing torches in my wake. Urged on by the men searching for me in the darkness with their lightsabers. And when they came close, I froze, flat and still in the water, my head cocked sideways so as I could breathe. Their torchlight washed over me, but I was hidden, bathed in mud and brambles. An invisible sludge boy.

'He can't have gone far! Find him.'

A multitude of frantic voices. Outwitted by a child.

The men came back and forth, shining their torches everywhere. Everywhere but me. The wind and rain shielded me. My allies.

Stay, Brandon. Hold … Lie low.

'He's nowhere, sir.'

An enraged voice broke through the storm. 'He has to be bloody somewhere, Foster. People do not just disappear! FIND HIM!'

Stay low Brandon … Stay calm …

The torches retreated to the top field and I continued my bramble gauntlet. I reached the end of the ditch and scrambled free. The men were nowhere to be seen as I darted across to the parlour, fighting my way home. My heart thumped inside my chest like a warhammer as I hugged the darkened walls, my brain awash with victorious desperation. I sprinted across the yard, through the barn, and into the chicken paddock.

Back to the safety of the farmhouse.

Or so I thought.

CHAPTER TWENTY-ONE

All-Out War

A tide of rain hit the farmhouse door as I slid across the concrete. I turned the key in the door and locked it behind me – fearful of the danger I'd brought with me. I threw off my shoes and filthy, sodden clothes and bundled them into a bag, then teased open the kitchen door and skidded across the kitchen.

In a flash, I was on Wrigley and cuddling in – my hands locked over his mouth.

'Quiet, boy. We're under attack.'

I shushed the big old dog several times until he seemed to have got the point. Then I slowly releasing my grip and hoped hard.

Wrigley was silent. Attentive. All ears. As if he knew something was going down. But he kept quiet.

'Come.'

I sneaked across the hall and prised open the dining-room door. Nana Biddle was fast asleep. *Good.* Tiptoeing back up the stairs, I avoided steps three and eight – the creaky ones!

I made it back to my room; battered, bruised, and cut to shreds by thorns. But I was safe.

I hurt all over, body and mind, but I was safe. With Wrigley beside me. My trusty canine guardian.

I jumped into the window bay, my heart beating in my ears. The view across the yard was unobstructed. The old windows did little to keep the storm at bay, and the plastic – Dar's pauper double glazing – created vacuums as the sheeting was sucked and blown with each new wave of the ferocious gale outside.

The hurricane had intensified. I must have been mad to venture into it. From the safety of my bedroom-window lookout, I looked at the yard below and across to the silhouette of the church in the village and beyond. Debris danced in the wind, and plumes of smoke rose from the lightning-scorched earth below.

And then I saw the white lightsabers!

Two men were hugging the shadows, their torch beams held low as they skirted the buildings and approached the house. A few barn roof tiles smashed to the ground, causing one torch and its handler to drop to the floor. Unfortunately, they missed. The man was promptly lifted by his friend and the beams continued towards the house. I wished the tiles had knocked them both dead … but I was never that lucky.

'I don't know what to do, boy!' My voice was small as I sought advice from Dar's old lurcher.

I'd disobeyed my grandfather and now I'd brought the bad men back. I took a moment to work things out, calming my breathing. Focusing my mind.

Were they dangerous? Or were they curious? Fact finders or stone-cold killers? I had to think. And fast. What would a Kriger do? What would a warrior do? *Think Brandon. Our very lives could depend on this moment.*

'A warrior would gather the troops!' I said to Wrigley.

I hopped down from the window bay, knelt and cuddled him.

'A warrior would stand up tall and, despite his fears, do what's right.'

He'd hold his head high, own up to his mistake and, no matter the trouble to come, take it, like a Kriger, on the chin.

And then he'd make it right.

I grabbed my tablet and left the room.

'Come on, boy.'

Wrigley followed as I entered Dar's room. I crept over to my grandfather and grabbed his shoulder. I shook him lightly, then less so.

'Wake up, Dar.' I shook him harder. 'Dar. Wake up. We're under attack.'

Dar stirred. His eyes opened.

'We're under attack. I'm so so sorry, Dar.'

He swung his legs out of the bed – instantly awake. Wrigley licked his face as he pulled on his slippers. He flicked on the bedside light, put his glasses on and stared at me.

'Dar. Two men with torches prowling the yard. Lackshaft's men.'

He rose and pulled on his dressing gown. I dragged him to my bedroom and towards the window.

'See anything?'

Dar sighed and knelt next to me in the darkness.

'You had a bad dream. Go back to sleep. It's the middle of the bloody night, boy.'

A sheet of lightning lit up the sky followed by an almighty crash of thunder. I hoisted myself up to the window as a huge tree fell through the chicken paddock, smashing one of the coops to mush.

'Wake up, Dar. Get your brain in gear. It's not a dream! There's men outside.' I flicked the light switch. 'Do I look like I've been asleep? Look. I'm sorry, Dar, but I went to the woods. I had to.'

He stared at me, adjusting his glasses – and his mind, no doubt, as he took in the evidence. I was covered in mud and all scratched up.

'I'm so sorry, I had to. And now I've brought this.'

Dar snapped to attention.

'Men you say. How many?'

'At least two. They grabbed me on my way back. I'm so sorry. I just wanted to take the dolls.'

Dar grabbed my wrist and led me downstairs.

'I wanted to give them to the twins so they wouldn't be scared. And to prove to you that I had what it takes to be Kriger.'

Dar ignored me as we tiptoed through the dining-room door.

'Nana's fine, Dar. She's asleep.'

We moved into the kitchen and Dar opened the airing cupboard. He punched the wall where Nana hung the ironing board and it sprung open – revealing a tall safe hidden in the wall. He dialled a code.

'Ever fired a gun, boy?' Dar pulled out a shotgun and lay it and a box of shells on the kitchen table.

'Millions of times … in games. But not … not for real.'

'Then you'd better have this.' Dar handed me a huge torch. 'A million candles. For lamping.'

He loaded a couple of shells into the gun.

'Do you know what lamping is?'

I shook my head.

'It's when you shine a light into a rabbit's eyes, to stop it in its tracks. Then you shoot it.' He paused and fixed me with a hard stare. 'Tonight, you're the lamper.'

He slung the gun across his back and handed me the torch. We snuck across the hall and back into the dining room.

'Wake your grandmother. Gently.'

Dar crept to the window and teased back the curtain. I shook Nana gently. She woke fast and bolted upright.

Then it was glasses on and out of bed in an instant. Her false teeth clattered as she pulled them from a glass on the bedside table and stuffed the into her mouth.

'Two up, Hilde. Maybe more. Southside. Clear on the back.'

Suddenly, my grandfather was a soldier. Floor-sweeping Dar was a thing of the past. Kriger Dar was growing before my eyes.

And it was epic!

Nana Biddle reached under her bed and pulled out a gun, like a cowboy one, like the *Lincoln repeater* from *Fallout 3*. It was almost as tall as her! Like a well-drilled soldier, she cocked it, checked for bullets, and snapped it back. Locked and loaded.

Damn, Old Whippet Legs was superbad. I never thought she'd sleep on a loaded gun like a wrinkly old Psammead badass. But there was my Nana Biddle, legs astride on her bed, stockings gathered around her blue-veined scabby ankles, steadying herself against the window. She squinted like a Wild West cowboy. Only a matchstick or a cigar between her teeth would have finished her badass look.

Dar pressed his face against the glass – looking out onto the back lawn. Nana had eyes on the yard.

'Light it up, Hilde!'

I watched in stunned silence as Nana Biddle fumbled behind her headboard.

Then the entire perimeter of the farmhouse was awash with light – a dazzling floodlight brilliance. Then came a siren – like the old Second World War ones – like a symphony in the storm.

'Top deck, Brandon. Eyes on!' Dar shouted as he peered through the window, shotgun in hand.

'Huh?' I said, wondering if somehow this was all a fantastical dream.

'Your bedroom. Perimeter check. GO!'

Dar was positively twinkling, alive with energy in the most badass way. I clocked Nana Biddle on the way out. She'd pulled her hair back with a curtain tie – now in full-on little old Rambo lady mode. I sprinted up the stairs in threes – followed by Wrigley – and jumped into the window bay.

Yard. Clear.

Orchard. Clear.

Barns and milking parlour. Clear.

I raced back down the stairs. Dar was gone. Nana had moved to the back-garden window. The storm screamed its rage through the open kitchen door. Nana pointed urgently towards the kitchen. I grabbed the huge lamping torch and stopped to give her a huge kiss.

'You, my dear old crazy lady, are pure badass. And I love you so very, very much.'

I ran to the back door, shielding my face from the bitter wind. Wrigley darted towards my bedraggled grandfather striding across the garden, gun in hand, in his slippers and dressing gown.

'DAR, WAIT.' But the howling wind sucked up my words.

I reached Dar's side just as an almighty fork of lightning struck one of the huge, ancient poplar trees that framed the garden. There was an explosion of smoke and fire, then the old tree creaked. It swayed as if undecided about which way to make its dramatic exit from the world – the latest casualty of Hurricane Zelda.

Dar braced himself and fired two shots into the hedge.

I shone my torch towards the gunfire. The giant circle of light illuminated a man as his silhouette leapt head-first through the trees. Car lights burst to life, and a large four-by-four roared down the lane.

Wrigley gave chase.

'GET BACK HERE!' Dar boomed.

Wrigley skidded to a halt and skulked back, head low. I grabbed his collar just as the sky lit up and a gargantuan thunderclap exploded directly above us. Wrigley yelped and bolted for the house, dragging me to the ground. Dar hauled me to my feet and I suddenly felt like we were playing out a level on *Battlefield 1*.

We fought our way back to the house through the storm – two bedraggled warriors in our pyjamas and dressing gowns, chasing down the bad men.

Lightning forked into the farmhouse, then with no more than a quarter of an elephant, *BOOM!* Thunder smashed the sky above, shaking us, and the ground below. Hundreds of tiles smashed to the ground. An orange fireball lit up the sky – a burning phoenix of flames, spewing through the gash in the farmhouse's roof.

We were in the thick of chaos. Apocalyptic chaos – the bright white light, the piecing siren, the howling wind and rain, and the most violent thunder and lightning I'd ever encountered.

The poplar creaked and ripped, adding to the symphony.

Time seemed to take a breather as, frame by frame, in super slow-motion, the tree toppled across the lawn towards us … and the farmhouse.

For a second, I imagined this was the end of us: the pyjama-clad warriors on the lawn. A boy and his Kriger grandfather about to bite it.

My hand found Dar's.

It was time to check out.

CHAPTER TWENTY-TWO

Farmageddon

The tree came down hard, smothering us. We were surrounded. My fists ached from the force of clenching them, from the terror inside that alerted me to IMMINENT DEATH.

But we were unharmed.

I stared at Dar, still perfectly upright. It was as if, at that precise moment, nature had decided to reward us for our bravery, the branches and leaves protecting us from the storm outside. Sheltering us from the carnage. As if we deserved our moment of respite.

Dar tugged my hand.

Through the branches, we emerged.

Unscathed. Back into the land of the living. Back into the eye of the greatest storm to hit England since 1986.

I staggered and followed Dar's gaze: his face pale and full of dread.

The huge tree had ripped through the roof, Dar's bedroom and the dining room, creating a chasm in the front of the house – like a wedge hacked from a block of cheese.

The dining room. Where we'd left Nana Biddle.

Dar was a few strides ahead of me by the time I'd collected my thoughts. Head down, fighting against wind, we raced towards the house. The security lights flickered among the sparks and flames.

Maybe you've played *COD*, *Medal of Honor* or other games where hell's being thrown at you from every angle … Imagine the utter carnage and put yourself right in the thick of it. And I don't mean comfortably at home with a can of fizz and a PS4 controller in your hand. I mean right in it. For real. Plucked up and tossed into the bowels of the apocalypse.

In the past I'd often wondered how I'd cope with something like this. It was part of my condition – worrying about the worst possible situations and obsessing over them. But at that point, I was frozen and terrified, and all that mattered was staying alive and rescuing Nana Biddle.

Flaming beams crashed through the ceiling, illuminating our path, as the fire engulfed the top floor. I reached the door, where Wrigley barked frantically, prancing back and forth, desperate to protect his master … yet wise enough to stay outside.

'DAR,' I shouted, but there was too much noise. From the storm, the thunder, the driving rain.

Think. Think. There's fire, flames, smoke. Cover your face. Need to breathe!

I grabbed a dish towel and stuffed it into the sink, then wrung out the dishwater and tied it around my face. It would have to do.

I found Dar in the dining room, or what was left of it, frantically lifting beams and debris in search of Nana Biddle.

'She's not here, Dar!' My voice was lost to the wind as Dar pushed past me and raced to the hall.

'Hilde! Where are you, my love?' He fought his way towards the menacing glow of flames, over broken beams and chunks of ceiling, and dragged himself up the stairs.

A ball of light, as bright as the sun, tore through the house.

BOOM. Another crash of thunder.

The house rattled in its foundations.

Part of the roof fell onto Dar, pinning him against the stairs. He roared as the impact knocked him to the ground, crushing his ageing bones against the stairs in the narrow gantry to the upstairs floor.

'DAR!' I jumped to his rescue, frantically pulling the pieces of house away from him.

'It's okay, boy. I'm not hurting. I'm trapped … but in decent fettle.'

He was pinned by a huge roof sleeper and a mountain of broken tiles.

'Go to Hilde. Go to your grandmother.'

I clambered over him, feeling my way up until I emerged at the top of the stairs. Fire painted the walls with light – orange, blue, green – as the wrecking-ball storm tore the old farmhouse to shreds.

'NANA! Nana, where are you?'

A scream turned my blood cold. I raced towards the sound – past my bedroom and to the bathroom. Nana Biddle cowered in the bath. She was covered in towels, coats and clothes.

'Good thinking, Nana.' I tried to sound calm even though my insides were twisted with terror.

Wood splintered, wind roared, electrics sparked and smoke closed in on us. I breathed deep and acted strong. 'Come on, Nana. Time to get you out. Are you hurt?'

I pulled her carefully from the bath. She was trembling.

'It's okay, Nana. I'll get you out.'

I held her close and pulled the bathroom door open. We were met with a wall of fire as the roof crashed down in front of us, blocking our way. I shielded her from danger and shut the door.

We were trapped.

The window was our only exit. Like the rest of the house, it had been built to last. Strong enough to survive an angry hippo, and perhaps even an apocalyptic storm. Diamonds of lead held the old glass in place like prison bars. I tried the latch. It was locked.

'The key, Nana! We need the key.'

Our eyes met for only the briefest of moments but we both knew there was no way out from the inferno.

Smoked curled through the space between the door and its frame, seeping into the bathroom like a dense fog. I grabbed a towel, ran it under the tap and draped it along the bottom of the door. It would buy us some time. Maybe a couple of minutes.

It wasn't enough. We had to act now. And fast.

I imagined Dar, shouting for help in the stairway, hideously trapped in the middle of all the horror with no idea what was to become of him. *Do something, Brandon. Be the warrior*, the brave voice inside my head screamed.

I kicked the towel rail off the wall. A huge ninja-kick, summoned from somewhere deep inside. *Smash. Smash. Smash.* Then I was pummelling the window with the rail like a sledgehammer.

The glass shattered but the lead held the broken panes in place.

SMASH! I forced the towel rail into a corner of the wooden frame.

SMASH! I prised open the corner.

I jumped onto the sink and kicked with all my might. Over and over again. The frame cracked, but the ancient wood held.

I ran back to the door and pressed my ear against it. 'DAR! DAR! Did you get out?' But I heard nothing but the taunt of the storm and the raging fire on the other side.

RIIIIP!

The sound was ear-splitting. The window was torn away from the wall and a huge hand appeared. Then a face.

Forfaltrot!

CHAPTER TWENTY-THREE

Fight or Flight

I touched Forfaltrot's hand, relaying my urgency. He instantly knew what to do. I lifted Nana Biddle to her feet and over to the sink. The huge troll grabbed her with one hand while I fed her legs through the hole, so the ripped wood and broken glass wouldn't tear her skin. And then she was gone – whisked to safety.

I was alone. Those few seconds cowering in the bathroom, were the most terrifying of my young life. The not knowing – that was the unbearable discomfort. I waited and hoped, hunched near the window hole, ready to jump. Preferably into the protective grasp of a troll, but, to the ground if I *absolutely* had to.

A moment later, Forfaltrot returned. I swung through the opening and onto his back, gripping the hair and foliage around his neck.

'Get Dar!'

Forfaltrot dropped to the ground then leapt around the house. His claws ripped into the concrete as he ran, eating up the ground as he carried out our desperate mission.

'Here!' I pointed to the wall and we skidded to a halt. The giant troll punched a hole through the brickwork, tearing away wood, plaster and cement until he'd burrowed an opening into the hall.

I pressed my face into Forfaltrot's back, sheltering from the dense smoke and vicious flames. We crawled towards the stairs, feeling our way through the rubble in search of my grandfather.

'DAR!' I shouted into the darkness.

Don't worry. I feel him safe, Forfaltrot thought to me, his words jumping straight into my brain.

Then Dar was being dragged by his legs as we reversed out of the house. The troll stretched upright and leapt onto the toolshed roof, spilling old tiles as his feet fought for a good grip. Then it was one gigantic stride onto the top of the muckheap, a jump across the machinery barn, and a leap onto the pylon post of the straw stack.

Forfaltrot punched his fist into the centre of the stack, showering bales around us and creating a straw cave in which to shelter. We swung from the pylon and splattered to a landing in the mud, my troll rock-steady on his giant feet. I nestled deep into his matted fur, sheltering from the storm as he scampered back up the pylon.

Nana Biddle, curled into the straw on the top of the stack, rose to meet us. Weary, shocked, drenched in mud and rain. But safe!

'Don't worry, Nana. We've got you. We've got Dar too. It's going to be okay now.'

Forfaltrot grabbed Nana Biddle, tenderly easing her down the pylon in his arms. Her tiny eyes widened at the sight of me, a rucksack boy on the back of his troll. Forfaltrot placed my grandmother in the straw cave next to Dar and gave them both a really deep sniff. I climbed down and approached my grandparents as Forfaltrot covered the entrance, sheltering us from the weather. A troll door.

Nana Biddle crawled over to Dar, softly sobbing, checking him over. She kissed his hand and recoiled as it slipped, lifeless, to the ground. He was so still. So, so, still. My grandmother cuddled into his chest and wept.

It was then that I realised.

Dar was dead.

I sunk to my knees. Not by choice – they did it all by themselves.

My eyes stung. I was empty. Numb. I hugged my grandmother, as she hugged Dar. There was nothing I could say.

Small mournful sniffles, almost a song – a terribly sad and haunting song – came from Forfaltrot. He rocked slowly as we wept. Nana sat upright, tears streaming down her face. She took my hand and placed hers on Forfaltrot.

I will heal him. If it is your wish, came Forfaltrot's voice, as clear as day inside my head.

Bring my darling back to me! Her voice was soft and calm in my mind. It was the first time I'd heard it and it forced a wave of pure emotion into the back of my throat.

Forfaltrot leant inside the cave, his bulk forcing me into the corner and filling the space with the stench of egg.

A stench heightened by a giant troll lick to my grandfather's face.

I shuddered as Forfaltrot bit the side of his own wrist. Huge pointed, vampire-like canine teeth sent a spray of red over Dar's face. Blood trickled from the wound and into my grandfather's mouth.

I touched Forfaltrot's hand.

Turn away, gods of the night. Make strong with blood. Bring life, bring birth. And rise again.

I felt the tears rolling down my cheeks. His voice was something from another world, soothing and peaceful. I focused on Dar, waiting for a sign. A glimpse of life, a glimpse of hope …

Forfaltrot roared.

Then he leapt, as if stung by a bee, from the alcove to the tractor-tyre mountain; a stone's throw from the stack. Stretching tall, and silhouetted by a halo of white light, he clutched at his back and roared into the sky.

I crept to the cave entrance, shielding my eyes from the super-bright sky, full of storm and rage. But now, too, the heavy mechanical whirring of a helicopter's rotor could be heard.

A helicopter hovered low in the sky, shining a huge spotlight down onto Forfaltrot. The engine choked and spluttered as the heavy metal bird fought to stay still amid the wind and rain – buffeted and lashed from all sides.

'AGAIN. RELOAD. SHOOT.' A loudspeaker broke through the wind. Through the open door of the helicopter, Lackshaft pointed wildly down onto our position, shouting instructions to his marksman.

No!

Forfaltrot had been shot.

And was about to be again.

I ran in front of the huge troll, waving my arms in the air like a madman.

'Don't shoot! Look, I'm a boy. I'M JUST A BOY!' My own safety was irrelevant. My amazing friend not getting shot was the only objective. I clambered onto Forfaltrot's back and straddled his shoulders, waving my arms at the helicopter.

We have to draw them away, I thought to Forfaltrot.

You must leave me now, he thought right back.

Hurricane Zelda toyed with the helicopter, boxing it around in the sky for kicks as the pilot fought for control. Wrapping his legs around the safety strapping, the marksman lined up another shot.

'DON'T SHOOT. I'M JUST A LITTLE KID.' I pulled out my mobile phone and opened the video recorder. 'I'M FILMING EVERYTHING! You can't just go shooting trolls,' I yelled into the wind, pointlessly wasting my voice as the marksman aimed.

Forfaltrot placed his hand on my shoulder.

Hold tight. Then the troll made a giant King Kong leap towards the helicopter, claws ripping at the air. He missed the fuselage by a whisker.

The marksman's eyes widened, shocked no doubt by the sight of a boy and his giant troll cannoning upwards towards him. All claws and teeth, ready to rip the helicopter to shreds.

'YOU DON'T SHOOT TROLLS!' I roared, pointing with rage at the man with the gun – as the helicopter swerved fiercely and almost hit the stacks.

Go. Head for the forest! I thought to my troll.

And he went.

The helicopter swooped after us and I held on for my life as Forfaltrot leapt onto the muckheap, and then onto the barn roof. He ran along the ridge of the building, jumping from roof to roof as the helicopter gave chase.

Through the barn, I thought. Forfaltrot followed my instructions and jumped down into the yard. *They won't come in here. They're not stupid enough to come all urban warfare on a troll.*

We crept towards the barn door. The helicopter hovered low in the sky and another gunshot rang out in the storm, splintering the wooden beam to my left.

Those evil cowards would have happily killed a child.

But not today.

We have to go. We need to make a dash for the forest.

I checked on the helicopter. A rope lowered to the ground and one of Lackshaft's men prepared to zipline down it.

We need to go now.

We burst through the barn door, boy and troll as one. Forfaltrot leapt onto the parlour roof and landed, in a spray of mud, on the track parallel to the orchard. We'd gained a few seconds on the helicopter. Before they'd realised we'd left the barn, we were out onto the open field, leaping at speed towards the safety of Pitchbury Wood.

And then came bright lights and chaos.

I shielded my eyes as two huge four-by-fours burst through the hedge. In a split second, they were beside us, hurtling across the field at maybe fifty miles an hour, trying to keep up.

And then everything stopped.

We dropped to the floor, downed by a huge net. Dazed and confused, we lay there, my troll and I, watching the two vehicles come to a stop. We'd been taken down like animals.

Forfaltrot rose like a wild beast, roaring and clawing at the men as they approached us. I was backed against troll and net as the men crept towards us, inch by inch, guns and flashlights on us.

Our game was over.

CHAPTER TWENTY-FOUR

The Pact

The whirr of helicopter blades filled the air. Through the net, I saw Lackshaft looming overhead.

'Good work, men.' His voice, raining down on us through the loudspeaker, sent a shiver of desperation down my spine. A cold and compassionless voice mingling within the raging storm.

I touched Forfaltrot's hand. *I won't let them take you.*

'LEAVE … US … ALONE.' Over and over again I screamed my warning as they inched closer to us.

I felt for my mobile phone and fumbled to open Facebook. 'IT'S RECORDING.' I held up the phone and stood defiantly between the troll and the men and their guns.

'My name is Brandon Ballard and I am a Kriger!' I filmed the helicopter, buffeting around in the air.

'SHOOT! Shoot the damned thing,' Lackshaft roared through the loudspeaker.

'GO ON,' I screamed. 'Shoot a boy, live on Facebook.'

The men were clearly taken aback.

'JUST SHOOT THE BLOODY THING!' Lackshaft yelled, his voice like ice, his intentions far colder.

'Go on then, shoot me! I dare you!'

Forfaltrot backed into the corner of the net.

Keep calm. They won't shoot, I reassured him. *They can't!*

God, I hoped I was right.

'SHOOT THE BLOODY CHILD IF YOU HAVE TO!'

The marksman raised his gun and I stood tall in front of Forfaltrot.

'So you're going to shoot a boy.' I grasped the rope net, staring deep into the gunman's eyes. 'You're going to kill a child. Somebody's son.' I imagined my dad watching in. If these were to be my last moments, they'd better count.

'For what? So you can destroy something else? So you can make some money? Kill me then.'

'SHOOT, GOD DAMN YOU, MAN!' Lackshaft's voice was urgent, drunk from the thrill of the hunt.

'Kill me. Because if this is the world then I don't want to be part of it.' And at that precise moment I utterly meant it.

A bolt of lightning, like a gift from the gods, struck the helicopter. A plume of black smoke billowed from the tail and it began spinning wildly in the sky. I watched as flames broke out and Lackshaft fell from the open door, hanging by his leg as the pilot fought for control. The helicopter rose high in the sky before spinning out of control towards Pitchbury Wood. It plunged into the trees. Then a loud explosion, followed closely by a ball of flame.

Lackshaft's men stood in silence, stunned. Squirrel Moustache lowered his gun and grabbed his radio.

'Sir. Sir. Come in, sir. Are you receiving? Are you receiving, sir?' Squirrel Moustache stared at his colleague.

Forfaltrot reached out and touched my arm.

'Let us go. We can save him. You need to cut us free,' I said, conveying the troll's words to Lackshaft's men.

The plume of smoke rose high above the wood, mingling with the wind and rain. 'We don't have much time. Cut us free.' I offered my mobile phone to the men. 'I've got no signal anyway. Cut us free. If your boss is still alive, we can help him.'

'Sir, are you receiving? Talk to me, Basil. Are you there?' Squirrel Moustache took a small knife from his pocket.

'Quick, we don't have much time.' I tossed my phone to the marksman. Lackshaft was probably already dead, and I didn't really care too much anyway. All that mattered was getting free, and this was our only way out.

The knife cut through our net easily. I jumped on Forfaltrot's back and he grabbed the marksman's gun and bent it double. The man cowered as the troll stretched tall, leaned into Lackshaft's men and roared in their faces — a monstrous bellow that forced them to their knees. I hoped they'd pissed themselves. That would be hilarious. Grown men wallowing on their knees in their own piss, at the mercy of a boy Kriger and his troll.

I grabbed onto Forfaltrot's hair, leaned in close and we set off across the field, towards the forest. I looked back. The two men sat on the ground, stunned.

The back end of the helicopter hung from the upper branches of a horse chestnut tree, the charred trunk still burning from the fuel. Flames licked the branches and showed us the way to the rest of the wreckage.

The pilot hadn't made it. I'd never seen a dead body before, and Forfaltrot shielded me from the full horror of the man's demise.

We found Lackshaft some way away from the wreckage. He'd obviously fallen from the helicopter before the explosion and landed in the trees.

It wasn't pleasant — he'd become fused with the tree courtesy of a particularly sharp branch. I know you have a good imagination, so I'll leave the rest up to you. But it sent a shiver down my spine and a little bit of sick into my mouth. I'll never look at a shish kebab in the same way again.

I rose up on Forfaltrot's shoulders and looked Lackshaft in the eye. He hung upside down, clinging onto the threads of life.

'Help me, boy.'

I stared at him. The giant tyrant now seemed incredibly small and helpless, despite his bulk. 'Please?' He coughed and rasped as he begged for my help.

'It's funny,' I said, laughing. 'Dar taught me that Gandhi said the weak can never forgive. And that forgiveness is an attribute of the strong.' I stared deep into Lackshaft's eyes. 'And the irony is, the troll blood you fought so bitterly, so cruelly to control … for all its power and healing … is the very reason you're dying now. That's what's funny. Because I'm just a kid.'

I stared hard at Lackshaft, remembering all the fear and pain he'd caused my grandparents. 'I thought I knew and hated the world – the greed, the bullying, the destruction, the hatred. But I wasn't even close to the truth. Because there are monsters lurking in the shadows. But it's not them we need to worry about! It's people like you, the guardians of the modern world. That's who we should fear the most.'

Forfaltrot turned away and we left Lackshaft hanging in the tree, living out his final moments with all the shame of the world etched into his face. We reached the old oak tree and I climbed down from Forfaltrot's back, staring behind me at the little speck of Lackshaft through the trees.

Forfaltrot rested his hand on my shoulder. A thousand years of peace and love coursed through my mind. It filled me with hesitancy and I stopped in my tracks.

But why? I thought back to him.

Kriger's strength is compassion. Rage begets rage. From compassion grows love.

I stared up at him, stunned.

Be compassion, Boy Kriger. And make a better world.

Forfaltrot lifted me onto his shoulders and we returned to Lackshaft. I stared deep into his eyes, seeing nothing but fear.

'I'm not strong. And I can't forgive either. But I'm Kriger, and I will learn.'

Lackshaft closed his eyes and his head dropped. My words had affected him. Forfaltrot lifted him from the spike and laid his body carefully on the forest floor. He bit into his wrist and fed the blood into Lackshaft's mouth.

The dense forest trees protected us from the raging storm outside, seemingly respecting the troll's compassion, whispering its appreciation. Forfaltrot spat on his hand and rubbed a gross mixture of eggy phlegm and earth into the wounds on the councillor's body. And then, before our eyes, the hole in Lackshaft's stomach disappeared, closing in on itself as if by magic. The colour in his face turned from deathly white to pink. It was like watching the coolest special-effects movie – skin, bone and flesh repairing itself, fusing back together. Like a lizard growing a new tail. Lackshaft's eyes fizzed back to life. He rose, reborn, and took a giant breath as his men closed in on us, guns raised and trained on our position.

'Lower your weapons.' Lackshaft grabbed my arm, pulling himself to his feet.

'Weapons down, men. THAT IS AN ORDER!' He faced his men, stretching tall, and allowing the healing troll blood to reach every last vein and sinew.

'Our work here is done. And if any of you speak of this day, ever, you and your families will disappear. Am I to be understood?'

'Sir?' Squirrel Moustache's handgun was trained on Forfaltrot as he edged closer, blowing hard, eyes wide and ready for the shot.

'Am I understood? FOSTER, you will not disobey a direct order … lower your gun, boy, or it's the end of you.'

The gun slowly lowered and Squirrel Moustache meekly handed the weapon to his superior. Lackshaft sighed and nodded slowly towards me. 'You win, boy.' Then he ambled towards the helicopter wreckage.

He located his briefcase in the strewn debris, patted out a small fire and pulled out the Ballard file, waving it towards me.

'Two hundred years of Ballard family ticks, crosses and details. It's all here, sonny.' He turned out the contents onto the fire and tossed the folder after them. 'And now it isn't. Come on, men. We've wasted enough of our time here.'

We followed them from the forest and back to the field where the four-by-fours waited in the driving wind and rain. Lackshaft clambered into one of the cars and slammed the door. The window slid open. 'Look after yourself, boy!'

'Does that mean my family are safe now?' I stared deep into Lackshaft's eyes. 'And the trolls?'

'Don't be stupid, sonny. You know trolls don't exist!'

The cars sped away across the field.

Lackshaft was gone.

CHAPTER TWENTY-FIVE

Boy 2.0

We rode back to my grandparents: a proud Kriger on his troll, returning to his people.

Nana and Dar had to be safe, just had to be.

Approaching the farm buildings, I noticed blue flashing lights mingling with the orange flames of the burning farmhouse. We clung to the shadow of the barns, keeping well out of sight. I peered around the corner. A fire engine crew tackled the blaze. Wrigley, barking furiously, was being dragged safely away from the wreckage by a nervous-looking firefighter, keen to stay away from the traumatised dog's gnashing jaws.

She led Wrigley towards an ambulance, tripping across the ground as the big old dog wasn't having any of it – until he spotted Dar and Nana Biddle wrapped in silver-foil blankets, sipping hot tea in the back of the vehicle. Wrigley leapt up, barging past the poor medic, and jumped all over Dar, licking him down with pure love and excitement.

Phew! They were safe. And very much alive. I didn't feel the urge to jump all over them and lick them half to death like poor old Wrigs … but a quick cuddle wouldn't go amiss.

I touched Forfaltrot's wrist, sharing a moment as we both rejoiced in Dar's return to life.

The fire hoses battled against the burning farmhouse. Beams, roof, walls, and my grandparents' possessions crashed to the floor as the crew fought to bring the fire under control.

But so what? It was just stuff. Forfaltrot had rewarded Dar with a troll's gift, *trollblod* – the healing elixir that had driven men mad with greed since the dawn of time.

I looked at my grandfather. He, like Lackshaft, was radiant with new life. Dar 2.0 was probably good for another hundred years or so.

It was time to return to them. And that meant Forfaltrot had to leave, too, for the sanctuary of Pitchbury Wood. To his family, to the anonymity of leaves, trees and the underground bunker that sheltered a secret known only to a few. We touched heads, Forfaltrot and I, sharing a moment of mutual admiration. A telepathy of confusing sadness, joy and respect.

And then he was gone.

Numb, I trudged towards the ambulance. Several paramedics descended on me, desperate to save a helpless child, wrapping me in foil blankets and forcing a hot drink into my trembling hands.

If only they knew.

Dar placed my hand in his as Nana embraced me, prickling my freezing cheeks with her chin stubble. We didn't say a word, just nodded gently to one another. I squeezed my grandfather's hand, glad beyond words that he was alive and well.

I sipped my hot tea as the fire crew tackled the blaze. Two black four-by-fours rolled by. I knew Lackshaft was in one of them because, even in silhouette, the man was a colossus. He flicked me a little salute as they passed. A salute of compassion for the boy Kriger.

You know, I thought saving the farm, my grandparents, their land and Forfaltrot would feel more … exhilarating. That I'd feel more alive, full of pride or smug about the whole saving-the-world thing. But to be honest, I was just tired and freezing cold. All that stuff – it's pure hassle, and I suddenly knew how Spiderman or Hit-Girl from *Kiss-Ass* felt. I was pure, bloody, knackered and just wanted to go to bed.

Hardly the heroic Kriger resolution, I know. I should probably have jumped onto the ambulance roof and screamed my name to the heavens or shined a Kriger signal at the moon or something. Just to give you, dear reader, that spine-tingling resolution you crave.

But that's not real. That's the fantasy world.

Me? I'm just a little bullied kid. One of the wheezy ones! We're everywhere! Fat ones, wonky-eyed ones, crooked teeth, braces, glasses, too much hair, not enough hair, wrong colour, no colour, bad breath, no breath … or maybe just that little bit too shy to function. Nobody prepares us for adventure. The world's quick enough to put us down, to tell us we're no good because we're different, or don't fit into the box. To fill us with insecurity, doubt and self-loathing.

You want my best advice? Just go for it. You might just surprise yourself.

But a quick, friendly word of warning. This hero thing, this standing up despite your fears, doing the right thing, saving lives and fighting for what's right … is totally bloody knackering. And it really, really takes its toll on the legs.

My name is Brandon Ballard, and I am the trollrider.

Did you enjoy reading *Trollrider*?

PLEASE LEAVE YOUR REVIEW ONLINE SO
OTHERS CAN EXPERIENCE BRANDON'S WORLD

You can also sign up for exclusive behind-the-scenes
goodies, and updates on forthcoming books in the series.

www.trollrider.com

Read on for a sneaky peek at Trollrider book #2

The Last Stand

BOOK #2: The Last Stand

by db Morgan

'A darker, and more adult magical-realism tale for YA
readers and the young at heart.'

  | The TrollRider

www.trollrider.com

233

Trollrider:
The Last Stand

PROLOGUE

Payback

Aiden Hunt had a boil on the back of his neck. Red, angry and ready to blow. I hoped it would explode and spit blood and pus all over his gleaming white shirt collar, because I couldn't deal with the fact that his shirt was nicer than mine. If I could have stomached hearing the sound of his toad-croak voice I'd have asked what washing powder his mum used. What brand of powder made his shirt so much whiter than mine. But then he'd just have said, 'F**k off Ballard. It's coz your mum's a p**s-head and can't afford to buy any brand names.' And that would have really p***ed me off … because he'd have been right.

I focused my Jedi mind power on the angry red boil, willing it to explode. Willing Aiden Hunt's whole head to explode. But it didn't. It just sat there on top of his rugby-player shoulders. A huge square head topped with ginger hair. Not bright ginger; faded but just ginger enough for people to make a point of it. Not that anyone made a point of it. People didn't pick Aiden up on anything. They just laughed at his cruel jokes, slapped him on the back and said,

'Good one, Aiden.' Like they were the best of friends. Dar would have called them sycophants. I called them sensible.

'BALLARD! What … is …. the quadratic … formula? I'm waiting boy!' Franklin tapped hard on the board with his ruler. He had an incredibly annoying voice. Especially when he thought someone in his class wasn't paying attention.

'I-I don't know, sir.' And I didn't.

'I bet your parents are extremely proud. Bravo!'

Aiden laughed, and his little gang of twats laughed along.

'Anyone else … Julian? … Well done. Simple really when you think about it.'

Julian could f**k right off!

Some time had passed since I'd returned home from the farm and things were pretty chaotic right now. Dar and Nana Biddle were in temporary accommodation because the farmhouse had burned to the ground. Mum was in bits at the end of a bottle because she couldn't grasp the reality of everything going on around her. And as for me, this was my first day back at school.

My hand felt the bump on my forehead. It had raised a good few centimetres since the last time I'd checked. I don't know how bad it looked but it felt like shit, and by the looks of the dent in my locker I'm sure there was to be some explaining to do when I got home.

Aiden caught me looking at him, but this time I didn't look away. Before, I'd have looked at my feet, or the wall

… anywhere just to get away from his gaze. But today was different. I held my gaze, waiting to see what came next. A little raise of my eyebrows. A narrow smile of defiance. A deep Kriger breath. Aiden sliced his finger across his throat, paired with the 'you're dead' mouth service.

And then … the storm!

I launched from my chair, sending it crashing backwards into Toby Williams, and charged, shoulder first towards Aiden. He rose to meet my challenge, jaw forward, shoulders hunched, all five foot seven of him braced for impact. Three years of torment coursed through my Kriger veins. Every hit, every taunt, every evil word channelled itself into my being. I was supercharged.

I caught Aiden low around the middle. My hands clasped together around his waist and my legs did the rest. We left the classroom floor beneath us. And then we flew.

The thud of Aiden's head on the concrete made a shocking sound. One, two, three punches to his eye. And then he was still. I sat up on top of him – my MMA ground-and-pound complete – shocked to see the blood all around us.

Blood and broken glass.

I looked up and around. It seems I'd taken him through the classroom window and down onto the quadrant below.

Maybe he was dead.

Maybe I didn't care.

CHAPTER ONE

The Darkest Place

Dad seemed rather upbeat considering I'd hospitalised his stepson.

'It's not that I don't like him. And I'm not saying he didn't deserve it either. But Christ, son. you've really done it this time. Why couldn't you have just told us? We could have helped.'

Dad turned up the car stereo. I turned it down again.

'Dad, please. I don't deserve this.'

'And you think I do?' he hissed. 'You nearly killed the kid.'

'Yeah, but I didn't … did I, Dad? He had it coming. He's a spiteful, evil prick. And you know that.'

'He's had it hard, Brandon.'

I couldn't believe my ears. Dad was actually defending him.

'You don't see him at home. He's not that bad. He's had a lot to adjust to.'

'And I haven't?' I said, my fury exploding. 'Didn't I have to adjust when you left on my birthday? Or when Mum was bashing her head against the walls because she couldn't deal with everything? Or when I had to hold William before he went to sleep every night because he wouldn't stop crying? What about me, Dad? Where were you then? Where we you when our world was turning to shit?'

Dad sighed deeply and turned the car stereo down.

'It's complicated.'

'You broke us, Dad. And you're only here now because … Actually, why are you here?' I felt a tear roll down my cheek and brushed it away with my sleeve, watching the moisture turning my new school jumper a shade darker.

Dad pulled the car into a layby.

'You were this close' – he pushed his finger and thumb into my face – 'this close from spending the rest of your childhood in *juvie* … in juvenile detention. I'm here because I'm supporting you. Let's have it right. Not pressing charges like Verity insisted I did. Pretty f**king strongly, I can assure you. I am keeping you in school. Me, Brandon! Not your mum. Not your bat-shit-crazy grandparents. Me! You nearly killed the kid …'

He grabbed the steering wheel and skidded out of the layby in a cloud of stones and dust.

We sat in silence and I watched the street lights fly by. Seventy, eighty miles an hour. I didn't really care. I'd never even heard of Ongar. I thought it was a type of eel.

'Will you stay for a while?' I rubbed Dad's hand on the gearstick. 'Help me … you know … get adjusted?'

'I don't know. I'm not sure they'll even let me. And I need to get back to the hospital. To Verity.'

Dad sighed and rapped his fingers on the steering wheel in time to his music. 'Thirty-six stitches, Brandon. How can I look your stepmum in the eye now?'

'Verity,' I corrected. 'She can hardly be my stepmum if I've never even seen her. I don't even know what your house looks like, Dad.'

'Well I'm marrying her, so that makes her your stepmum. So don't be a smart-arse. It doesn't suit you.'

'So can I spend my first leave weekend with you then?'

Dad scoffed. 'Yeah, coz that'll be cosy. Tell you what, you can spoon-feed her son through the neck brace while we're all watching *EastEnders*.'

'Now who's being a smart-arse?' I said. 'What would you have done?'

'Exactly the same as you, son, except I'd have done it years ago. But that's why I drive a cement truck for a living and sell tiles at the boot sale every bloody weekend. I expected so much more from you. You're smart. And if you're telling me you had no other choice then I've got to believe you. And I'm sorry I wasn't there to make it right.'

'But?' I could sense one coming.

'But I'm with Aiden's mum. So you tell me, son … what the hell am I supposed to do?'

I shuffled uncomfortably in the car seat. Too anxious about what lay a few miles ahead to give it much further thought.

'I don't know, Dad. You do what you need to do.'

Elmbridge Boarding School was ancient. The big wrought-iron gates led towards an old, ivy-covered building that looked a bit like Kentwell Hall. We had a meeting with the headmaster at eleven-fifteen and were already late. I couldn't really see much of the main school from the front but, by the look of things, it wasn't too shabby. I hadn't had much time to work out how I felt about switching from my old school to Elmbridge, but it couldn't be worse than that shithole, and I'd kind of burned my bridges there since I'd pole-axed Aiden through the year-ten maths classroom window.

Dad passed my suitcase from the back of the car. 'What did your last slave die of?'

'Sarcasm!' I grabbed the case and slammed the boot shut.

Mister Davenport, the headmaster, had the eyebrows of a maniac. He looked over my file, whiffling little grunts and whimpers as he got to know my paper self rather than the real me sitting opposite him.

'Dear me. You have had a bit of trouble. Bright, good results. Aaahh … working well above your expected levels in science. Good. You'll get on well with Mr Marfleet. "Can do better" appears to be the running theme.'

The headmaster looked at me across the brown leather-topped desk, peering through his glasses down the length of his nose like they were crosshairs on a gunsight. 'You don't appear to be too troublesome. Are you troublesome?'

'No, sir. I'm not.'

'He was pushed. To the limit.' Dad took the lead as I sat looking at decades of school photos on the headmaster's walls. You know the ones: the whole school line-up with teachers at the front. But these were empty faces. Not the standard ones from a normal school, where a hundred fake bunny ears appeared behind every head and making stupid faces was expected. It was a line-up of ghosts. Drones. A thousand kids who missed their cats, essential home comforts and the security that came from a loving parent.

'He's a good boy, Headmaster. But there's only so much a child can take. And he knows he's very lucky not to be in a whole world more trouble. Isn't that right, son?'

I nodded.

'We run a tight ship here at Elmbridge, Mr ...' The headmaster checked my records. 'Shefford. Parents entrust their children to us from far and wide to benefit from our disciplined approach to education. And they leave as well-rounded young men, well equipped for the rigours of life and all that comes with it.'

He pointed to a wooden crest on the wall. *Labor omnia vincit.* Hard work conquers all.

I suddenly a very bad feeling.

An hour later I'd put my clothes in *my* wardrobe and all my other gear in a wooden locker under my bed. I was the only kid in the dormitory, or dorm as everyone kept referring to it. I stared with confusion at what was to be my bed for the next three years. The dormitory windows looked onto the sports field and I could hear the draft whistling through the old metal-framed windows. Behind the formality of the fancy headmaster's administration building things had certainly lost their gloss. My dorm room was basically a large wooden shed, one corner of a concrete tennis quad with three other wooden buildings in each corner. I noticed a bit of scrubbed-out graffiti on one of the wardrobe doors: *We're doomed, I tell ya. Doomed.*

It seemed pretty appropriate as I lay on the bed and tested the mattress, feeling somewhat lost.

244

Tell your mates about Trollrider. They'll thank you for it.

www.trollrider.com

-db- Morgan